HOME FOR THE MURDER

Also by Theresa M. Jarvela:
Home Sweet Murder

HOME FOR THE MURDER

Theresa M. Jarvela

NORTH STAR PRESS OF ST. CLOUD, INC.
St. Cloud, Minnesota

First Edition: June 1, 2013

Printed in the United States of America

Published by
North Star Press of St. Cloud, Inc.
P.O. Box 451
St. Cloud, Minnesota 56302

www.northstarpress.com

www.northstarpress.com · Facebook - North Star Press · Twitter - North Star Press

Footprints of my

journey

across the

shores of

life

are washed away

beyond the tides

of time.

*For my family and friends who fill my life with warmth,
laughter and sandcastles.*

CHAPTER 1

Meggie Moore bent over a bed of bright rosy purple chrysanthemums. She snipped one and laid it in the basket she carried on her arm. "Walter can't go to Key West with me." Meggie brushed a scattering of highlighted tendrils from her face and snipped again.

"What are you going to do?" Shirley Wright, plump and short in stature, stood nearby. "Who's going to housesit for Stella and David if you don't go?"

"I'm still going." Meggie arched her slender back. "Ouch. It hurts to bend anymore."

"No way you're going." Shirley's voice cracked. "You're pulling my leg."

Meggie laughed and looked down at Shirley's legs. "I don't think so." She held a large mum next to her friend's tunic top. "The name is Grape Glow." Meggie tilted her head. "Almost a perfect match, isn't it?" She handed the flower to Shirley, crouched down and snipped several more. "There's still time to change your mind and come with me."

Shirley sniffed the mum. "Like I said before—an invitation containing the words 'Meggie' and 'housesit' gives me the chills."

Meggie stepped around the bed of mums and gazed at the profusion of flowers in bloom. She brushed past Shirley and sauntered down the brick footpath. A squirrel scampered out of her way and ran up a nearby maple tree.

Meggie understood why Shirley didn't want to go to Key West after what happened during the housesitting job on Spirit Lake. It had been a bad experience for both of them.

Shirley caught up to Meggie. "And I suppose it doesn't bother you that Stella's house has been broken into not once, but twice?"

"The guest cottage was broken into. Not the house." Meggie handed the basket of mums to her friend. "And that was before they bought it." Meggie watched a chickadee light on the birdfeeder that hung from the birch tree beyond the flower garden. It picked up a sunflower seed in its beak and flew to a nearby lilac branch.

"What's the difference?" Shirley said. "Besides, I hear it's anything goes down there. It's not like Minnesota where we keep our clothes on." She paused. "I hear they run around naked and paint their bodies."

Meggie threw her head back and chortled. "That's Fantasy Fest and it's not in September." She fingered the tall pink gladiolus. "And not everyone runs around in their birthday suits during Fantasy Fest, either."

"So what's Walter's excuse for not going?" Shirley flicked a pesky fly from her shoulder. "What did he retire for if he's not going to be available when you need him?"

Meggie cut a large glad stem and held the flower to her nose. "His bucket list."

"His bucket list?" Shirley's eyebrows shot up. "What's he doing with a bucket list?" she asked. "That's the most original excuse I've ever heard." She fanned her face with her hand. "Walter should go, you know. Your odds would be better."

"Odds?" Meggie frowned. "What do you mean my odds would be better?" She clipped another glad stem.

"Your odds of not ending up dead or maimed or accused of murder." Shirley's eyes grew large. "That's what I mean by 'your odds would be better.'"

"Honestly, Shirley." Meggie gaped at her friend. "Sometimes I think you're rowing up a river with one paddle."

"I could say the same for you. Face it, Meggie." Shirley rested her hand on her hip. "How many times have you housesat?"

"Two times." Meggie narrowed her eyes. "And I know where you're going with this."

"Hear me out . . . it's for your own good."

Meggie lifted her hand, palm up.

"And how many times have you found a dead body while you're housesitting?" Shirley took a deep breath and answered the question. "Both times."

"Those murders had nothing to do with me or the fact I was housesitting." She snipped four more glads. "I just happened to be at the wrong place at the wrong time."

"I know." Shirley smirked. "And bodies happened. I rest my case."

"You think this will be enough?" Meggie held several gladioli up for Shirley to see.

"Don't change the subject."

"Mmm." Meggie squinted one eye. "What was the subject? I forgot." She held the bouquet of glads and watched a yellow butterfly flit from flower to flower.

"What is Walter doing with a bucket list?" Shirley paused. "Is it some kind of secret or something?"

There was nothing secretive about Walter's bucket list but it irritated Meggie that Shirley needed to know everything. Besides being nosy, her friend took top prize for being persistent. But whether Meggie wanted to or not, she knew sooner or later she would tell Shirley all about Walter's bucket list.

Meggie and Shirley, both baby-boomers, had been friends since high school. Over the years Meggie wondered more than once how they remained such good friends. Shirley could be downright annoying. On the other hand, she could always count on Shirley when she needed her. *Friendship*, Meggie thought. *Now that's a mystery.*

"Let me clip a couple more flowers." Meggie stepped in front of Shirley. "Then we'll go inside and have some iced tea."

Shirley feigned disinterest and fluffed her pixie haircut.

"And I'll tell you all about Walter's bucket list."

Shirley's face lit up. "Good. I could use a strong cup of tea." She surveyed the garden. "You know," she said. "I have to admit you've done a nice job here." She waved her hand around the garden. "And I love that picket fence."

Meggie smiled when she thought about how hard Walter worked on the weathered picket fence. After he pounded the last nail he told her he had finally fenced her in after thirty years of marriage.

"I don't know where you find time for all this." Shirley interrupted Meggie's thoughts. "I think I would be tempted to spend my time right there." She pointed to the three-season gazebo in the center of the fenced-in area. "I wouldn't have so many flowers." She smiled. "But I'm thankful you do. How else could I supply the church with so many beautiful bouquets?"

Meggie wondered if Shirley had the right idea. She would like to spend more time inside her gazebo but there weren't enough hours in the day. She thought about her part-time job at Hearts and Flowers Gift Shop.

"How about that purple one over there?" Shirley scooted along the brick path. "The ladies are just going to love these pink gladioli," she said. "Can we have a bouquet of purple glads, too?"

Meggie clipped five white and three purple glads. "How's that?"

"Wonderful. They'll look great with the bouquet of purple mums."

Meggie chuckled.

"What's so funny?" Shirley asked.

"Too bad I don't have orange." Meggie grinned. "Or maybe lime green with yellow and pink polka dots."

"So what if I like my colors bright?" Shirley spoofed offense. "Bill says it gives me an aura."

"An aura?" Meggie laughed. "Let's go inside and have that tea." She led the way out of the garden and pulled the gate shut behind them. "I think you've been in the sun too long."

Meggie took a stool from the entryway closet and set it on the floor in front of the kitchen counter. She reached into the top shelf of the cupboard. "You'll need something to take the flowers home in." She set two glass vases on the counter. "Don't forget to return these."

Shirley wrinkled her nose. "Of course I won't forget." She lifted the lid on the cookie jar and peeked in. "What do you have to go with the tea?" she asked.

"You won't find anything in there," Meggie said over her shoulder as she took the iced tea out of the refrigerator. "I've cut down on my baking."

Shirley pulled in her stomach. "Whatever for?" She opened a canister on the counter and closed it.

Meggie poured two glasses of iced tea and carried them to the table. "Walter actually started losing weight and I don't want to sabotage him."

"I wish Bill would gain some." Shirley's hand reached for the bread box.

"You're getting very warm."

"Huh?" Shirley flipped the bread box open.

"That's a fresh loaf of rhubarb bread," Meggie said with a grin. "Would you like some?"

"Thought you'd never ask." Shirley handed the loaf to Meggie. "Tell me you made it and not Marjorie Winkman," she added flippantly.

Meggie pointed to herself and wondered if Shirley and Marjorie would ever call a truce.

"I'd like to know who told that woman she could bake," Shirley said.

Meggie set a plate of sliced rhubarb bread in front of Shirley. "Didn't she win a prize for her rhubarb bread at the fair?"

"Ages ago, but the judging was rigged." Shirley helped herself to a slice of bread, slathered butter across it and took a bite. "Mmm." She sat back in her chair and looked at Meggie. "Let's have it," she said. "What's that husband of yours up to now?"

Meggie squeezed a slice of lemon into her tea. "Remember I mentioned Walter was having a hard time since he retired?"

Shirley nodded. "About 1,001 times." She passed the sliced rhubarb bread to Meggie.

"Even with his part-time job he has a lot of down days."

"You mean he feels old." Shirley popped another bite of bread into her mouth. "Is he still losing sleep over his little bald spot, too?"

Meggie laughed. "I suppose. A little bit." She broke her bread in half. "He feels like he's over the hill and sliding down the other side."

Shirley pushed the ice in her glass up and down.

"He enjoys his part-time job at the Legion Club." Meggie shrugged her shoulders. "But lately he's been having life regrets."

"Life regrets?" Shirley tapped the side of her glass. "What do you mean?"

"Life regrets. You know. Things you regret not doing during your lifetime."

"Oh, those kind of regrets." Shirley looked out the window towards the back yard. "I suppose we all have a few of those."

"So when a friend at work suggested he make a bucket list, he jumped on it."

"All right, so he's got himself a bucket list." Shirley refilled their glasses and set the pitcher down. "Sounds to me like a good way to get out of what he doesn't want to do and not feel guilty." She shook her head. "I hope he doesn't give Bill any crazy ideas about a bucket list." She paused. "What's on this bucket list that's so important he can't go to Key West with you?"

"Well, for starters," Meggie began. "You know he's always wanted to hunt small game in South Dakota."

Shirley lifted her chin.

"This is the year for the small game hunt in South Dakota." Meggie averted her gaze. "He's already formed a hunting party."

Shirley's eyes narrowed.

"He couldn't back out now even if he wanted to." Meggie lifted her hands, palms up. "He doesn't want to, anyway."

"And who comprises this hunting party of his?" Shirley arched an eyebrow. She set her glass of iced tea on the table and leaned back with her arms folded across her chest.

Meggie opened her mouth to speak.

"Please don't tell me Bill's in the party."

"Uh-oh." Meggie cleared her throat. "He didn't mention it to you, did he?"

"No, he didn't." Shirley spit her answer out. "When are they leaving?"

"The seventeenth of September." Meggie looked down at the table. "I'm sure he planned to tell you."

"I'm sure he did." Shirley carried her glass to the sink. "In his own good time."

Meggie knew Shirley hated it when Bill kept secrets but she hated it more when she discovered his secrets from someone else. She knew her friend was peeved and Bill was in for it.

"Thanks for the flowers and snack." Shirley picked up a vase. "I think I better get home."

"I'll carry this one." Meggie picked up the second vase and followed Shirley to the car. "Let me find something to set them in." She rummaged in the garage and found a cardboard box. She set it on the floor in front of the passenger seat and placed the two vases inside. "That should keep them from tipping."

Meggie watched the red Taurus barrel down the driveway while the finger of guilt poked at her. She shouldn't have let the cat out of the bag. On the other hand, Shirley would have found out about the hunting trip sooner or later.

Meggie's tomcat, Peppie, wrapped himself around her leg and looked up, as if to say *I told you so*. She bent down and stroked his head. "It's not my fault she didn't know about the hunt." She shrugged. "Bill should have told her himself."

CHAPTER 2

LATER THAT AFTERNOON, MEGGIE sat on the deck and watched the birds in the backyard. A cardinal glided to the ground under the large free-standing birdfeeder. It hopped around and pecked at the fallen bird seed.

Meggie felt lazy and mentally counted the items on her to-do list. She looked at her watch. Walter told her he was scheduled to close the Legion so he wouldn't be home until late. She decided to have an early dinner and take a walk afterward. She pushed herself out of the chair.

Peppie waited in the house on the other side of the sliding screen door. He looked up at her and meowed. She reached down and rubbed his back. "Hungry?" She found a can of cat food in the cupboard and set it in front of him. On her way to the refrigerator the phone rang.

"Yeah, it's me," Shirley said. "When are you leaving for Key West?"

"Second week in September." Meggie shooed a fly off her arm.

"I've changed my mind." Shirley sounded defiant. "I'm taking Stella up on her offer."

"You're sure?"

"I'm sure."

"I don't have to ask what changed your mind." Meggie knew Shirley was retaliating against Bill.

"No, you don't."

Meggie ended the call and thought how excited Stella would be. It had been over three years since their friend divorced and moved from Bluff to Key West. She had remarried and found happiness, but she missed her friends.

THE NEXT MORNING AT BREAKFAST Meggie told Walter what transpired the day before.

"You mean he didn't tell her himself?" Walter smirked and shook his head. "It doesn't surprise me. Shirley can be a pill." He cupped his camouflaged coffee mug. "Maybe he planned to tell her at the last minute so he didn't have to listen to her nag."

"Be nice," Meggie said. "I'm happy she changed her mind. I'll have more fun if I have someone to travel with." She knew Walter didn't want her to housesit or travel alone.

"You know how I feel about you housesitting," Walter said. "Not to mention the fact you'll be over 2000 miles from home." He paused. "In Key West of all places."

"Don't worry about us," Meggie said. "We'll be fine."

"I sure hope so, and if you get yourself in a mess don't count on my help. You'll be too far away." Walter pushed his plate back.

Meggie didn't bite Walter's bait. "I've called Stella and she's going to let me know as soon as she gets the tickets."

"What day are they leaving on the cruise?"

"September 17, but she wants to hang out with us before she leaves so we're flying into Miami a few days early."

"Miami?"

"We plan to rent a car and drive to Key West." Meggie smiled. "This might be our only chance to see the Keys."

Later that day Meggie printed out the itinerary for her flight to Key West and noted the early departure from Lindbergh Terminal. She made a motel reservation near the Minneapolis/St. Paul International airport and logged out of the computer.

Meggie decided to take a walk when the phone rang. She answered it and walked to the recliner. "It's Bud." She gave Walter the phone and left by the front door. Halfway down the driveway she decided to go back to the house and get a visor.

When she reached the house, she found Walter on the front steps. He had his camo cap on his head and his truck keys in his hand. She looked at her wristwatch and up at him. "Are you going somewhere?"

"Somebody broke the lock on Bud's shed again." Walter shook the keys. "I told him I'd pick up another lock at Ace Hardware before they close and run it out to him."

Meggie's stomach clenched. "Did they take anything?"

Walter shook his head. "It would probably make him feel better if they did." His face flushed. "Pure harassment, that's all it is."

CHAPTER 3

MEGGIE'S ALARM BUZZED at 6:30 a.m. Instead of hitting snooze like usual, she pushed the alarm button and jumped out of bed. She had a few last-minute things to do before she left for the Twin Cities and she didn't want to rush.

"Good morning." Walter greeted her from the recliner. "Today's the big day."

Meggie smiled and poured a cup of coffee. She walked past the big screen TV and looked out the bay window onto the street. "It looks like it's going to be a nice one." She watched a black squirrel scurry up the oak tree and disappear. "What's the forecast for today?" She waited for Walter to reply. "Yoo-hoo . . . did you hear me?"

Walter's eyes were glued to the television set. "What did you say?"

"Never mind." Meggie pulled her robe close to ward off the chill and walked to the kitchen. "Have you eaten?"

"Yeah, I've been up for a while," Walter said.

Meggie hurried through breakfast and took a shower. She stood in front of the mirror and carefully applied purple eye shadow to accent her green eyes. She leaned into the mirror, touched the corner of her eye and noticed the crows had been at it again. She sprayed on her favorite perfume and snapped her make-up bag shut.

In the bedroom she checked her travel list. Satisfied she hadn't forgotten anything, she zipped her suitcase and carried it into the front room.

"I'm running into town for a bit," Meggie said. "I need to stop at the bank for cash and I told Vera I'd swing by the shop to say goodbye."

"What time will you be back?" Walter asked. "You know we have to leave about noon."

"I told Shirley to be ready by 11:30 so she won't be late." She gave Walter a peck on the cheek and waved goodbye.

Meggie parked her Volkswagen Bug in front of Hearts and Flowers Gift Shop in downtown Pine Lake. Owner Vera Cunningham stood near the greeting cards and appeared to be by herself. The bell tinkled above the door when Meggie entered the shop.

"Hello, dear." Vera, a spry lady in her seventies, reached up and placed a homemade greeting card in the rack. "I'm so glad you could make it." She smiled, smoothed her hair and tucked it into the bun at the back of her head. "Eldon will be here shortly."

"I'm so glad he volunteered to help out while I'm away," Meggie said. "You'll be in good hands." She knew Eldon Kellerman liked to spend time with Vera and vice versa.

"The ladies do a splendid job on these recycled cards." Vera stood back and examined the card rack. "A lot of work goes into them."

"You said something about Nettie's embroidery pieces?" Meggie had no idea where Vera planned to show them since the little shop bulged at the seams. "Should I bring in that small shelf unit we have in the back and display them on that?"

"Yes, why don't you?" Vera patted Meggie's arm. "That's a wonderful idea."

Meggie returned with the unit and set it up. She took the embroidery pieces and arranged them on the shelves.

Vera stood nearby and dusted the collection of hand-painted loons Francis Johnson delivered earlier that morning. "Are you excited about your trip to Florida?"

"Yes, I'm very excited . . . all packed and ready to go."

"I'll say a prayer for a safe flight." Vera quit dusting and smiled at Meggie. "And an extra prayer that your housesitting experience will prove much more enjoyable than the last two."

Meggie appreciated Vera's concern. "Thanks. I'm sure everything will be fine."

"Do be careful down there. One doesn't know who to trust anymore," Vera said. "Times have certainly changed and it's a different world we live in today." She dusted the tiny head of a miniature loon. "It's a shame, really." She shook her head. "I remember the day when you didn't need to lock your doors at night and neighbors looked out for one another."

Meggie hugged Vera and assured her she would take care of herself and Shirley, too.

"I know you'll enjoy your time in Key West," Vera said. "Eldon and I will be thinking of you."

CHAPTER 4

THE ALARM BUZZED BESIDE THE BED and chased away Meggie's dream. It took her a moment to realize she was at the motel in Bloomington. She rolled over, squinted at the clock radio, and turned the alarm off. She heard singing and sat up.

Meggie padded to the bathroom and stood in the doorway. "What time did you get up?" An unfamiliar sweet scent hung in the air.

"Early. I couldn't sleep." Shirley primped in front of the bathroom mirror and fluffed her hair. "I guess I must be more excited than I thought."

"It's 3:30 a.m. and you're already dressed?"

Shirley turned toward Meggie. "How does this look?" She plopped a cherry red hat on her head and the wide brim flopped around her face.

"It matches your outfit." Meggie cocked her head and took a long look at the hat. "Looks like you're ready for some fun in the sun. Where did you hide that?"

"It's one of those hats you squish and it bounces back." Shirley took it off her head. "Look, it's reversible." She turned it inside out. "Now it's yellow."

"I like it. Actually, it looks good on you." Meggie stretched. "Now, can I use the bathroom?"

Shirley stepped outside the door, bent over and swept her hand toward the bathroom. "Madame, the water closet is all yours."

When Meggie finished in the bathroom she found Shirley with her back to the full-length mirror. "Are you still looking at yourself?"

Shirley held a small mirror in her hand and examined her backside. "Does my butt look big in these pants?"

14

"It doesn't matter. You don't have to look at it."

"You're a big help," Shirley said. "But I suppose you're right."

Meggie folded her nightgown and put it in her carry-on. She stuffed her toiletries into her beach bag.

Shirley waited by the door. "Anytime you're ready."

Meggie turned off the wall light and slung her beach bag over her shoulder. "Guess I have everything." She looked around the room. "Shall we?"

CHAPTER 5

MEGGIE AND SHIRLEY STOOD on the curb under the American Airlines sign and waited for the shuttle driver to unload their luggage. The terminal's automatic glass door slid open. Wheeled luggage squeaked by and a horn honked. The shuttle driver pulled out the last two pieces of baggage and set them down in front of Meggie and Shirley.

"Look at the long line." Shirley struggled to keep pace with Meggie. "I hope we don't miss our flight." She wheeled her bag to the end of the security line that snaked inside the rope-enclosed area.

Meggie glanced at her watch. "We have plenty of time."

"I still don't understand why we need to take our shoes off." Shirley ogled the passengers going through security check. She watched them remove outerwear and shoes.

"It's for our own good." Meggie slid her boarding pass into the ID wallet that hung from her neck.

Shirley showed her identification and set her bag on the conveyer belt. She bent over, removed her sandals and tossed them in the bin. She leaned toward Meggie and whispered, "I suppose it won't be long until they ask us to remove all our clothes."

"That would be scary," Meggie said.

Once through security, they proceeded to the gate. After a short wait, a cheerful middle-aged woman picked up the microphone and announced they would begin boarding.

Meggie stood in the aisle in front of their assigned seats and slid her carry-on into the overhead compartment. Shirley squeezed by her, plunked down in the window seat and adjusted her seat belt. "I can't bear to sit squinched up in the middle." She settled back. "You don't mind, do you?"

Meggie preferred the window seat and it had been assigned to her, but she obliged her friend and sat down in the middle seat. "No, you stay there."

Shirley jabbered through take-off and until they were airborne. "And I told Audrey I was glad you talked me into taking this trip. She knows how long Stella has wanted us to visit her." Shirley lowered her voice. "I also hinted she should think about being more spontaneous." She kicked her personal bag under the seat in front of her. "You know I don't like to harp on anything, but that woman needs to loosen up a bit. She's been widowed well over two years."

Meggie turned the page in the mystery novel she held in her lap. "Audrey has always been shy. You know that." She marked the page in *Dead Man's Float* with her finger and looked at Shirley over her reading glasses. "She opened up a lot this past year. You know she never liked your matchmaking."

"She doesn't know a favor when she sees one." Shirley held her hands up and checked her painted nails. "Did you say Stella and David rent out their guest cottage?"

"Bud Anderson's grand-nephew rents it."

"That makes me feel better." Shirley's head fell back against the seat. "It's safer that way."

Meggie rolled her eyes. "Safer?"

"I promised myself after what happened at Spirit Lake I'd never get involved in one of your housesitting adventures again." Shirley opened her eyes and looked at Meggie. "But here I am winging my way to Key West with you. Go figure." She cupped her hands around her head and appeared to twist it. "Is my head on straight?"

"I hope you don't throw that little episode up at me this whole trip," Meggie said. "Or I'll be sorry I asked you along."

"Little episode?" Shirley laughed. "Meggie, you look at the world through rose-colored glasses."

Meggie never cared for take-off and landing and secretly rejoiced for the non-stop flight Stella booked them. Once the plane cruised at high altitude she settled back and read most of the way. They had been in the air for almost three hours when the pilot announced their descent.

"Seventy-five degrees in Miami," Shirley said.

"I can't wait." Meggie tucked her novel inside her beach bag and glanced out the window. "I hope the weather lasts.

The plane rolled to a stop and passengers pulled their cell phones out, turned them on and began to chatter. The seat belt sign flashed permission to unbuckle. Travelers crowded the aisle and overhead compartments sprung open. Meggie removed her seat belt and inched her way into the aisle.

Shirley scooted out and attempted to reach the overhead compartment. A distinguished-looking man with a swarthy complexion took hold of Shirley's bag and set it down in front of her. He smiled and reached in for Meggie's bag. "There you are, ladies," he said and walked past them to the front of the plane.

Meggie watched a red blush creep up Shirley's face. She turned to exit and felt a poke in her back.

Shirley leaned forward and whispered in her ear. "I think this is going to be one heck of a trip."

CHAPTER 6

THE RED TWO-SEATER CONVERTIBLE sped down Highway SR-821 South toward Key West. Meggie sat behind the wheel and glanced up at the cloudless blue sky. She leaned back in the bucket seat, inhaled the salty air and let the sun's rays penetrate.

"Hey." Shirley shouted against the wind.

Meggie tipped her head to the side. "Huh?"

"We're not in Kansas anymore." Shirley laughed and held her hat down. The brim flopped up and down. "How long will it take to get to Stella's?"

"About three or four hours from Miami." Meggie's eyes were riveted on the road.

"That long?" Shirley watched the cars whiz by them. "Everyone's passing us."

The baby blue ruffles on Meggie's top fluttered in the breeze. "I'm going the speed limit." Her words were lost in a current of air.

"What did you say?" Shirley's hair blew into her eyes.

Meggie pointed to the speedometer and raised her voice. "I said I'm going the speed limit."

"If you drive this slow we'll never get there." Shirley shrugged her shoulders. "Oh well," she raised her voice. "Far be it from me to tell you how to drive."

In less than an hour Meggie turned off SR-821 S onto Highway 1. The ocean shimmered as far as the eye could see. "It's gorgeous." Meggie glanced at Shirley. "This southernmost leg of Highway 1 is known as the Overseas Highway."

"Sometimes called the Highway That Goes to Sea," Shirley said. "Bet you didn't think I studied up on Key West, huh, professor?"

Meggie grinned.

Shirley took out a pack of Doublemint gum from the pocket of her crop pants. She opened a stick and offered one to Meggie.

"Guess not. Maybe we can stop for a bite to eat soon?"

"I didn't want to complain but I'm famished."

"That makes two of us."

Shirley looked dumbfounded. "Come to think of it, we haven't eaten much today. How much further to Is . . .la . . . mor . . ."

"Islamorada." Meggie pointed to a road sign up ahead. "Not far."

Shirley squirmed. "It depends on your definition of far."

"Seventeen miles isn't far." Meggie arched her eyebrows. "You won't starve by then, will you?"

"I suppose not." Shirley wiped the back of her neck. "But if you can step on it a bit I'd appreciate it. I have to go to the bathroom."

The sign on the side of the road announced Islamorada. "Let's eat at that fish place." Shirley jabbed her finger toward a restaurant on the side of Highway 1.

Meggie tapped the brake and turned into the parking lot.

Shirley whipped her seat belt off. "Just in time, James." She jumped out of the car and dashed inside.

After a bowl of conch chowder, Meggie and Shirley got back in the car and continued their journey.

Shirley pointed to a road sign. "Approaching Key Deer Habitat."

Meggie knew Key Deer were an endangered species and slowed down to forty-five miles per hour.

"I had no idea there were so many Keys." Shirley snapped a picture of a sailboat bobbing on the water near Little Duck Key.

The red Miata purred down the highway past the mile markers and soon entered the city limits of Key West. Meggie slowed the car and coasted to a stop in front of a red light. She shaded her eyes against the afternoon sun. "What was that address again?" She peered at the name of the cross street.

"Too bad you forgot the GPS." Shirley's reading glasses hung on her nose. "1401 Black Street." She lowered the printed MapQuest directions. "Would you look at that?"

Meggie glanced at Shirley. "What's the matter?"

Shirley nodded toward the crosswalk. "Her cup runneth over."

Meggie shushed her friend and watched a young woman in a skimpy halter top cross the street in front of them. "She might hear you."

"A person sure sees everything down here." Shirley smoothed her tank top. "Go. The light's green."

Several minutes later the red two-seater pulled up in front of a pale yellow house with white trim. Meggie fell back in the seat. "We're here. That's a load off my mind."

"Look." Shirley pointed to the picket fence. "Almost like yours."

"It's lovely, and look how intricate it is." The pickets abutted each other, their tops a lacey cut-out design. "And the house is so cute."

Shirley threw off her seat belt, pulled down the visor and fluffed her hair. "I'm ready."

Meggie didn't see anyone about. "Maybe they're not home."

"There's one way to find out." Shirley crawled out of the car and slammed the door.

A tall slender woman on the upper deck turned her head.

"There she is." Shirley pointed toward the rear of the house. "Stella!"

"Hello. I'll be right down." Stella held onto the stair rail and hurried down the wooden steps. She made a beeline toward them and wrapped them in a bear hug. "It's so good to see you."

"You look wonderful, Stella." Meggie stood back. "Key West agrees with you."

Stella brushed short wisps of hair from her tanned face. The haircut accentuated her high cheek bones and large blue-gray eyes. "Thank you. I feel wonderful." She stood back. "And look at you. Young as ever." She gave Shirley a mischievous look. "I'm glad you changed your mind about making the trip."

"That makes two of us." Shirley looked at Meggie. "I mean three of us."

"Come on in." Stella draped her arms around them. "David's waiting."

Meggie and Shirley marveled at the open front porch that spanned the width of the house. A white wicker porch swing with blue-speckled cushions sat to the right of the front door. A matching rocker faced the swing. Potted plants, a testament to the balmy weather in the Keys, were scattered here and there throughout the porch area. A lovely Hibiscus tree in full bloom stood at the far end. Its bright orange-red flowers drooped in the sultry air.

The front door swung open and startled Meggie. "Come in. How was your trip?" David, a tall man with kind eyes, held his hands out in welcome and motioned them inside.

Shirley went into animated detail about their drive.

Meggie tuned her out for a second and thought about David and how youthful he looked.

Shirley poked her. "Don't you think so?"

Meggie realized she had been staring at David and lost track of the conversation. "What did you say?"

"I said this is a lovely house."

"We think so." David winked at Stella and turned back to the girls. "What can I get you? Would you like a drink?"

"A drink sounds good. Surprise me with anything wet and wild," Shirley said.

David turned to Meggie. "And you, do you want to be surprised?"

"I love surprises," Meggie said.

After Meggie and Shirley called Walter and Bill to let them know they had arrived safely, Stella led the way upstairs. "Let me show you where you'll be sleeping."

Meggie thought the house had personality. The carved wooden stair rail had been painted white and the walls along the staircase a soft green. There were two bedrooms, a sitting room and full bath upstairs.

"This is the larger guest room." Stella pushed the bedroom door open.

"It's charming," Meggie said as she stepped into the room.

A four-poster bed stood in the center of the room, surrounded by pale yellow walls. A border of white daisies circled the room near the ceiling. Meggie fingered the white crocheted bedspread. "What a beautiful piece of work."

"It belonged to my mother," Stella said. "I've always loved it."

"This room has Meggie written all over it," Shirley said.

Stella pointed out the bathroom and moved on to the door beyond it. "And this is our smaller guest room." The walls were papered with deep violet flowers against a white background splashed with green.

Shirley seemed quite taken with the room.

"The deck runs from this bedroom to the corner of the house," Stella said. "The guest rooms are used very little. David's children visit occasionally, but Brian rarely visits." She smiled. "We were thrilled when he offered to relieve you from housesitting for the last part of our trip."

David called from downstairs to let them know their drinks were ready.

"We'll be right down." Stella motioned Meggie and Shirley to go first.

David set the drinks on the table next to the sofa and offered to bring in the luggage.

Meggie reached into her bag and handed him the keys. "There are only two. We travel light."

The four friends did a lot of catching up and soon their glasses stood empty on the table. David looked at his watch and suggested dinner at a Spanish restaurant he and Stella enjoyed. He held his hand up. "Don't worry. You have an hour to freshen up."

Later that evening Meggie opened the French door in her bedroom. Moonlight streamed over the picket fence and onto the hedges and palm trees. A slight breeze skimmed her face. She closed her eyes and felt a peace, a lightness. "I am definitely not in Kansas anymore." She inhaled a floral scent. *I feel ageless*, she thought. *It must be the Keys.* She chuckled to herself. *Or the Chardonnay.*

Meggie's eyes rested on the guest cottage almost hidden from view. An ominous feeling crept over her and her skin tingled. She shook her head. *It must be the Chardonnay.*

CHAPTER 7

THE EARLY MORNING SUN FILTERED through the curtains. Meggie opened her eyes, stretched and looked at the bedside clock. Her plans to sleep in the first morning of vacation hadn't gelled. She threw the sheet back and slid out of bed.

Meggie hoisted her suitcase onto the bed and started to unpack. She carried her outfits to the closet and folded the smaller items and placed them in the dresser drawer. When she finished, she carried the empty suitcase to the closet and pushed it to the back corner.

A knock startled Meggie and she pulled the bedroom door open.

"Good morning," Shirley said in a low voice. She leaned on the doorframe dressed in a bright yellow tank and yellow crop pants. "I wasn't sure you'd be up. I could hardly sleep last night." She spun around. "How do I look?"

"Like a lemon drop."

Shirley grimaced. "No, really."

Meggie chuckled. "Like a cute lemon drop, then." She tapped her lip, tilted her head. "You sparkle."

Shirley posed. "I do, don't I? I wonder if Stella is up yet."

A clang bang sounded downstairs. "Someone is." Meggie threw on a cover-up and closed the door to her room. "Let's go down and see."

"Good morning. You're up early." Stella stood in the kitchen near the counter dressed in a full-length pink nightgown. "We weren't sure if you'd sleep in this morning or not."

"I slept like a log and rose with the sun." Shirley sat down at the table. "I think Key West agrees with me."

Meggie thought about Walter's snoring. "I had the best night's sleep in years."

"Would you like some coffee?" Stella took two mugs out of the cupboard. "Sit down and make yourselves at home."

"I love this cozy kitchen." Meggie pulled her chair close to the table.

"Here you go." Stella set two coffees in front of them. "If I remember right, you both like it black."

"We do," Meggie said. "Is it always so quiet here?"

"Most of the time." Stella glanced out the screen door to the back yard. "You've probably noticed how close the houses are." She looked at Meggie and Shirley. "We were fortunate to find a home with such a large lot."

A timer buzzed and Stella picked up two potholders. "I'm fixing you breakfast. David is running errands. When he gets back he can follow you to return the rental." She removed a tin of muffins from the oven. "I hope you still like Mandarin orange muffins." She set them on a wire rack to cool.

"They're one of my favorites." Meggie recalled the first time she tasted Stella's muffins. The three of them and Audrey had met at Pine Lake Park early in the morning on the day of the annual craft fair.

"You bet we still like them," Shirley said. "Do you need some help, Stella?"

Stella placed the muffins and a plate of bacon on the table. "No, just relax." She set a pitcher of juice in front of them and refilled their coffee cups.

After breakfast Stella gave them a tour of the yard. She led the way out the kitchen door onto a ground level porch.

"You can pick and choose the porch you sit on," Meggie said. "I suppose with weather like this you're able to make the most of all three."

Stella nodded. "Speaking of weather, it's so good of you to come down this time of year."

"This time of year?" Meggie didn't understand what Stella meant.

Stella bent over a delicate, odd-looking red rose. She inhaled and peeked up at Meggie. "Hurricane season."

"Hurricane season?" Shirley halted.

"Don't worry." Stella waved her hand. "You'll have several days' notice if a hurricane is spotted." Stella looked from Meggie to Shirley. "There's really nothing to worry about. We've never had to evacuate."

"Evacuate!" Color drained from Shirley's face. "Oh, my gosh. What do we do? Where do we go?"

Meggie had given no thought to hurricanes. Minnesota had its share of storms—blizzards, floods, tornadoes—but never hurricanes. She knew it wouldn't do any good to worry about something that might never happen.

"Before we leave, David will go over everything with you in case there's an emergency."

"That makes me feel a whole lot better," Shirley mumbled.

A fuchsia-colored plant grew near the picket fence. "What kind of flower is this?" Meggie lifted a bright bloom.

"That's a bougainvillea." Stella waved her arm. "They grow all over the Keys."

"It's so bright and cheerful."

"What's with all the chickens running around down here?" Shirley asked.

"Key West Gypsy Chickens, but that's a long story," Stella laughed. "I'll save it for later." She led them to a large heart-shaped swimming pool near the back of the lot and opened the gate. Beach chairs were lined up on both ends with small metal tables snugged up beside them. A palm tree near the far end of the pool swayed in the breeze.

"That's our guest cottage." Stella nodded toward a vine-covered building. The white cottage trimmed in yellow sat beyond the swimming pool. "I told you we're renting it out to Ronald Davis." Stella looked at Meggie. "He speaks highly of his great-uncle Bud." She rubbed her arm. "I doubt if he's up or I'd make introductions. He's the same age as Brian. Twenty-eight."

"I know Bud and Lydia but I don't believe I've ever met Ronald." Meggie wondered about Stella's connection to the young man. "Did you know Ronald when you lived in Minnesota?"

"He played with Brian when they were kids." Stella kicked a rock with her foot. "He lived in St. Paul but visited family in Bluff during the summer."

"I know Bud and Lydia have a brother in St. Paul." Meggie watched a yellow butterfly flit past Stella. "He must be Ronald's grandfather."

"Arvid. Ronald's mother, Caroline, died in a car accident when Ronald was in high school." Stella shaded her eyes. "He never knew his father."

"How did he end up here?" Shirley asked.

"Brian hadn't heard from Ronald in years and one day he received a friend request from him on Facebook. They got together a couple of times in St. Paul and a short while later Ronald closed his facebook account. Brian didn't hear from him again until he moved to Key West."

"He called you out of the blue?" Shirley asked.

"Ronald had been looking for a different place to live and Brian mentioned we might rent the cottage." Stella shrugged her shoulders. "David and I wanted to rent it out so we told him he could move in."

"Does he work?" Meggie walked beside Stella.

"He bartends at Finnegan's. They have good food and a nice atmosphere." Stella motioned for Meggie and Shirley to follow her. "Let's go inside. I have some brochures for you to look at."

Stella set a stack of tourist pamphlets on the table. "Here you go."

"It looks like we'll have plenty to keep us busy," Shirley said.

Meggie and Shirley studied the pamphlets until David came home. He asked if they would like to return the rental car.

"Good idea." Shirley pushed her chair back. "I better grab my purse and floppy hat."

"I'll get them," Meggie offered. "I'm going upstairs anyway."

When Meggie returned, David, Stella and Shirley were waiting outside for her. She joined them on the porch and had a pleasant surprise. Behind the rental car sat a small silver car with the top down. "Is that yours?" Meggie looked at David, then Stella.

Stella laughed. "It's yours for the duration of your stay." She pointed to the car port. "If you need a bigger car you can use the Malibu."

"This is just too much." Shirley clapped her hands. "I can't wait to tell Bill. He's going to be so jealous."

CHAPTER 8

SUNDAY MORNING DAVID LOADED the luggage into the trunk of the red Malibu and climbed into the driver's seat. He and Stella planned to fly out of Key West into Miami and from there catch an afternoon flight to Venice, Italy.

"I'm so excited for you." Meggie buckled her seat belt. "I wish we could have spent more time together. Three days wasn't long enough."

David adjusted the rearview mirror and started the car. "You'll be back. Try to talk Walter and Bill into coming with you next time."

"I'm going to put a cruise on my Christmas list this year." Shirley lowered her voice. "Not that it'll do any good."

Meggie gazed out the window at the activity around her.

"What I wouldn't give for a trip to Venice," Shirley said.

Meggie turned toward Shirley and noticed a dreamy look wash over her friend's face.

"And a cruise of the Eastern Mediterranean and Greek Isles," Shirley continued.

"Put it on your bucket list," Meggie teased.

Shirley's face lit up. "What a great idea. I'll start a bucket list."

At the airport David unloaded the luggage. Meggie and Shirley hugged Stella and wished her *bon voyage*.

"You have our itinerary." David gave Meggie and Shirley a hug. "You know how to get in touch with us if you need to." He looked at Stella. "You ready?"

Stella and David entered the terminal but before they were out of sight David called over his shoulder. "Don't forget about Robert the Doll."

Shirley slid into the front seat and turned to Meggie. "Who's Robert the Doll?"

"He's at the Fort East Martello Museum." Meggie pulled away from the curb and related what David told her about the Fort's Key West history. "I'll show you the museum." She drove a short distance and nodded her head toward an old brick building. "It's right there."

"I like museums. Let's go in."

Meggie hesitated but turned into the parking lot. "We should tour it, I suppose. It's part of Key West's history."

On the way into the museum, Meggie told Shirley the story of Robert the Doll. "And according to legend, if you want to take a picture of Robert the Doll you must politely ask his permission. If he tips his head to one side, permission is denied. If you take the picture anyway, the doll will curse you and your family."

An hour later Meggie and Shirley stepped out of Fort East Martello Museum and into the sunlight.

"Ewww. Robert the Doll gave me the creeps." Shirley shivered and looked back at the museum. "I wonder if there's any truth to the legend?"

Meggie shrugged. "You'll find out." She widened her eyes and lowered her voice. "You took his picture."

"I know. And I didn't ask him politely." Shirley crossed her arms. "I'm not about to ask a stuffed doll for permission to take his picture." Shirley stroked her eyebrow.

Meggie took her time driving back to the house and before long turned off Flagler Avenue onto Black Street.

"That doll isn't going to curse me or my family." Shirley threw off her seatbelt.

"Are you still thinking about Robert?" Meggie laughed and killed the engine. "Let's go inside and make some vacation plans."

Shirley sat at the table and poured over Key West brochures. "It seems strange without Stella and David around." She picked up a pamphlet. "It was nice of them to take us on the glass-bottom boat cruise."

"It was fun." Meggie pushed her chair back and walked to the refrigerator. "Do you want some lemonade or something?"

Shirley set the pamphlet down. "Lemonade sounds good."

Meggie set two glasses of lemonade on the table. "Hand me some of those, please." She sat down. "I'll help you look."

Shirley's head hung over a rather large pamphlet. "Oh, my!"

"What did you find?"

"Ghost tours." Shirley shivered. "I'm not sure about that one." She handed the brochure to Meggie. "What do you think?"

Meggie sipped her lemonade. "Wooo. The Original Ghost Tours of Key West."

"How about this?" Shirley waved another pamphlet at Meggie. "Let's take a tour of the Ernest Hemingway House."

Meggie set the ghost tour brochure onto the "maybe" pile and the Hemingway tour on the "yes" pile. A charter cruise advertising snorkeling had worked its way to the top of the pile. Meggie slipped it underneath the bottom brochure. "Here's what I think we should do." She sat back in her chair. "Let's count our money and see how much we have to work with."

"That sounds like a plan."

"Then we can make a list of those things we really want to do."

"I better not spend too much." Shirley's voice was flat. "I wouldn't want to give Bill a coronary." She flipped over another brochure. "It looks like there's plenty to do without spending an arm and a leg."

An hour later three piles sat on the table. Meggie tossed a book of coupons down on the "yes" pile. "What do you say we get on the bikes and ride towards Mallory Square?"

"Bikes?" Shirley's eyes bulged. "Are you serious?"

Meggie stood and took her glass to the sink. "We can do a little shopping and find a nice place to have lunch."

Shirley picked up the pamphlet on snorkeling.

"What do you think?" Meggie asked.

Shirley cleared her throat. "I'm thinking the last time I rode bike I broke my ankle." She tossed the pamphlet on the "maybe" pile.

"Oh, come on," Meggie coaxed. "Be a sport."

Shirley crossed her arms. "And do you remember how I hobbled around for months?"

"It'll be fun." Meggie's eyes spoke mischief. "I promise if you get tired we'll come back and get the car."

"All right." Shirley followed Meggie out of the kitchen. "I don't know why I let you talk me into these things."

"Because we're such good friends," Meggie said on her way up the stairs.

"I can't tell you how many times that fact has gotten me into trouble," Shirley said. "Not to mention the time I almost lost my life."

"You only risked your life . . . *really* risked your life one time." Meggie stopped near her bedroom door.

"You're keeping count?" Shirley shook her head and mumbled, "I can't believe you."

Meggie felt guilty because in a roundabout way she did feel responsible for Shirley's involvement in Louise Benedict's murder. But they both risked their lives in proving their innocence. For Meggie, that episode was over and done with, ancient history, but Shirley had a difficult time letting go.

Meggie opened the closet door and slipped her sandals off. She carried her tennis shoes to the small chair next to the French door and pulled them on. She took cash and her ID out of her purse and stowed them in her camera case. Downstairs she found Shirley waiting on the porch swing.

Shirley glanced at her watch and stood up. "I hope you know where you're going." She rubbed her tummy. "It's almost lunchtime."

Meggie locked the front door and dropped the key into her camera bag. She led the way to the carport and disappeared inside a small shed next to it. She wheeled a large two-wheeled bicycle out and leaned it toward Shirley. "They have big tires and foot brakes," she said. "I'll ride David's."

Shirley tilted her head and took hold of the handlebars. "An old-fashioned bike. This might not be so bad."

Meggie walked back into the shed and returned with David's bike. "I don't think we have far to go." She adjusted the bike seat and set her camera bag in the basket.

"Don't forget I have low blood sugar." Shirley wheeled her bike to the gate.

"How could I forget?" Meggie lost track of the number of times Shirley mentioned her low blood sugar.

Shirley swatted her arm. "Darn no-see-ums. I'm glad Stella warned us about them." She scratched her arm. "At least you can see mosquitos. Not these cowards." She led the way through the gate. "Remember, I can't exercise vigorously if I'm hungry. I'll get dizzy."

Meggie tried to recall one time her friend exercised vigorously but couldn't. "You'll be fine." She closed the gate behind her. "Ready?"

"And I sure don't want to take a spill if I can help it." Shirley straddled the bike and adjusted her back pack. "I'm glad Bill talked me into bringing this backpack. He checked online for things to do down here and suggested I use it to keep my hands free."

"Good thinking on his part. It's much easier to ride a bike."

Shirley's lip curled down. "He was being sarcastic. He knows I like to shop." She set her right foot on the pedal and pushed down. The bike jerked ahead and wobbled. Shirley yelled over her shoulder. "He likes to make fun of me."

"You're always thinking the worst." Meggie threw her leg over the bike and caught up to Shirley.

Mallory Square teemed with people—shoppers, sightseers, young people and old people. Meggie walked her bike beside Shirley. "What do you say we lock these bikes and have some lunch?" They came to a bike rack a couple minutes later. Meggie slid her bike in, locked it and waited for Shirley to do the same.

"All done." Shirley brushed her hands against her legs.

Meggie took a notepad out of her camera bag and studied a list. "Here are some of Stella's suggestions for lunch."

"How about we try that place over there?"

Meggie put the notepad back into her camera bag. "Fine with me."

After lunch, they paid the check and left. They walked a short distance before Meggie remembered her camera. "Hold it." She held her hand in front of Shirley. "Let me take your picture." She fished her camera out of the bag.

Shirley fluffed her hair. "Where do you want me to stand?"

"How about over there?" Meggie pointed to a small shop with vintage clothing in the window.

"It reminds me of the '60s." Shirley walked to the front of the shop, carefully avoiding a scruffy looking panhandler standing nearby.

Meggie adjusted the camera, held it to her eye and waved her hand to the right. "Over a little." She didn't want to include the panhandler. "Say Key West."

Shirley's smile spread across her face. "Key West."

Meggie snapped the picture.

"Would you like me to take a picture of the two of you?" A middle-aged man dressed in jeans and a tee shirt approached Meggie. "Maybe you could take our picture afterwards." An attractive brunette stood back, wiggled a small camera and smiled.

"Thanks." Meggie handed him the camera. "That would be great."

The stranger took their picture and handed his camera to Meggie. She snapped a picture of the two of them.

"How did our picture turn out?" Shirley asked.

Meggie peered into her camera. "Great picture of the three of us."

"Three of us?"

Meggie pressed the button to display the picture and handed the camera to Shirley. "You, me and the panhandler with the red bandana."

Shirley held the camera in front of her. "I don't have my readers on so I can't see it very well." She handed the camera back to Meggie and laughed. "If the picture isn't good we'll blame it on Robert the Doll."

CHAPTER 9

LATER THAT EVENING MEGGIE LOUNGED on the deck outside her bedroom. She squeezed a slice of lime into her rum tonic and took a sip of her drink. The moon hung high in the sky and sent beams shooting across the swimming pool and over the bougainvillea near the picket fence. The air carried a sweet smell, laughter and music.

Meggie glanced at the guest cottage hidden behind the foliage and hanging vines. The glass windows glowed with reflected moonlight. She thought about Ronald and made a mental note to introduce herself the next day. She rested her head against the lounge chair and closed her eyes. A warm breeze stirred and caressed her face before her mind drifted off to sleep.

Sometime later a horn honked and Meggie sat up. The moon had disappeared behind the clouds and the yard lay in darkness. She picked her drink up, swished the diluted liquid and pushed herself out of the chair. She glimpsed a light flicker near the cottage, pressed her eyes together and opened them. She looked at the cottage again but it stood shrouded in darkness. She scolded herself for imagining things, carried her glass into the bedroom and closed the French door.

Meggie pulled her nightgown over her head and considered ways to approach Ronald the next day. He had an odd schedule and that's why they hadn't crossed paths. But she knew the time had come for introductions. If she didn't see Ronald during the day, maybe Shirley would agree to dinner and drinks at Finnegan's.

No longer tired, Meggie picked up her book and pushed thoughts of Ronald from her mind. She pulled the bed covers back, crawled under the sheet and opened *Dead Man's Float*. She read until her mind became jumbled and the book fell from her hand.

CHAPTER 10

A LOUD KNOCK AWAKENED MEGGIE the next morning. She sat up and rubbed her eyes.

"Hey, you alive in there? I'd say it's time to get yourself out of bed, girl." Shirley stood in the doorway with a floral printed apron tied around her neck.

"I'm on vacation," Meggie stretched her arms over her head. "That's why I didn't set my alarm."

"It's 10:00 a.m." Shirley looked impatient. "Early morning swim, remember?" She tapped her foot. "We can make it if you hurry."

"I'm getting up now."

Shirley crossed her arms and waited by the door.

Meggie looked at Shirley. "I'm getting up now."

The door closed for an instant, then swung open. "Breakfast is ready!"

Breakfast? Meggie guessed Shirley must have rolled out of bed early. She smiled at her friend's enthusiasm and recalled her reluctance to make the trip in the first place. She slid off the bed and pulled the covers back into place. She reached into the second drawer of the dresser, found her aqua-colored swimsuit and slipped it on. The beach towel Stella left for her lay on top of the dresser. She stuffed it in her beach bag along with her cell phone and sunscreen.

Now that she was up, she felt anxious for the day to begin and hurried out of the room. The aroma of fresh-brewed coffee tickled her nostrils and drew her into the kitchen. The table was set and the juice poured. "Wow, you've been busy."

Shirley stood at the kitchen range. She dished up a plate of scrambled eggs and carried them to the table. "I'm slaving, you're sleeping." She slipped out of her apron and laid it across the chair.

"What can I do?"

"Dish up the sausage."

"Yes, ma'am." Meggie saluted and set the sausage next to the eggs. "Anything else?"

Shirley pointed to a chair. "Sit." She walked to counter and picked up the carafe.

"What a treat." Meggie pulled her chair close to the table. "Thanks."

"You're welcome." Shirley handed a cup of coffee to Meggie. "Just don't say I never did anything for you." She sat down and pointed her fork at Meggie. "Is that a new suit?"

"No." Meggie took a bite of sausage. "I just haven't worn it much. It's last year's clearance special."

"I like it, and the color looks good on you."

Shirley wore a bright orange swimsuit with a large red hibiscus splashed across the front. "You look pretty fashionable yourself."

"I bought this half-price." Shirley tugged at the shoulder strap. "It was the last one in my size." She took a bite of scrambled eggs. "How does everything taste?"

"Great." Meggie's forehead creased. "But we might have to wait before we go into the water after eating all this food."

"It's a pool, Meggie. Not a lake in Minnesota." Shirley wrinkled her nose. "I'm not sure I believe all that stuff about cramps, to be honest with you." She pointed to herself. "It would take a mighty big cramp to sink me."

After Meggie finished eating, she set the dirty dishes in the dishwasher.

Shirley wiped her hands on the kitchen towel and jerked her head toward the back door. "We're outta here."

Meggie grabbed her beach bag and stepped off the back deck into the bright sunshine. She tilted her head back, looked up and didn't see a cloud in the sky. "Isn't the sun wonderful?"

"Yes, it's wonderful." Shirley strode toward the pool. "And I'm overdue for some fun in the sun."

Meggie bent over a spindly rose bush and drew in its fragrance. She followed after Shirley and watched her open the gate to the pool area.

"This is going to feel—oh, my gosh!" Shirley yanked her sunglasses off and drew her hand to her chest. She stared at the pool.

"What's the matter?" Meggie rushed towards her.

"There's a body floating in the swimming pool!"

The man's body floated face down, its arms outstretched. The smell of chlorine permeated the air and the water had taken on a murky color.

"We can't just stand here." Shirley turned to Meggie. "What do we do?"

There was no question the man was dead, and they couldn't save him. Meggie rummaged through her beach bag and pulled her cell phone out.

"911. What is your emergency?"

"There's a dead man floating in our swimming pool." Meggie pressed the phone closer to her ear. "Black Street . . . 1401 . . . Meggie Moore." Meggie repeated the address to the dispatcher and answered several more questions. In the distance she heard a siren wail.

Shirley backed away from the edge of the pool, sat down on a pool chair and put her sunglasses on.

The sirens grew louder. Meggie disconnected the emergency call and clutched the phone to her chest. She watched the body bob up and down and wondered if time had run out for introductions.

CHAPTER 11

MEGGIE AND SHIRLEY CLIMBED the steps to the Mattson's porch. It had been a grueling day at police headquarters and the temperature had risen steadily and now registered eighty-five degrees.

Shirley plunked down on the porch swing and wiped her brow. "Well," she said, "I can't say it surprises me." She kicked off her shoes and pushed the swing with her foot.

Meggie sat on the wicker chair across from Shirley and rocked back and forth. "What doesn't surprise you?"

"The dead body." Shirley crossed her arms. "You and dead bodies seem to be a thing."

"Don't be silly," Meggie countered. "It's pure coincidence that Ronald was murdered while we were here."

"Friend, I have one thing to say," Shirley sat forward in the swing. "MYOB."

Meggie didn't say anything but kept rocking.

"For both our sakes please mind your own business."

Meggie didn't care to point out the fact to her friend that she wasn't the one who found the body. She glanced toward the cottage. The crime tape had been taken down. She wondered if they had discovered any clues in their search. "Did you hear anything unusual last night?"

"No. I slept like a baby." Shirley lowered her eyebrows. "Why?"

"I just thought you might have heard something." Meggie thought back to the previous night when she thought she saw a light in the cottage. "I wonder what they found in the cottage."

"I don't know and if you were smart, which most times I think you are but then again . . ." Shirley shrugged and rolled her eyes. "You'd quit wondering. It's bound to get you in trouble."

"I don't understand why I didn't hear the gunshot," Meggie said. "The window was wide open."

"It's none of our business." Shirley threw up her hands. "Don't go making mountains out of—"

"Molehills." Meggie finished. "In a way it *is* our business."

"Right. We're persons of interest." Shirley grimaced. "Been there, done that."

"We have nothing to worry about. I'm sure they'll clear our names."

The conversation turned to plans for the next day—the tour of the Ernest Hemingway House and Museum. When Meggie suggested lunch at Sloppy Joe's, a saloon frequented by the author, Shirley agreed.

The afternoon passed quickly and neither Meggie nor Shirley was hungry at dinner time so they settled for a snack. Early in the evening, Shirley complained of the headache of a lifetime and apologized to Meggie for leaving her with the clean-up. "I think I'll call Bill and then I'm turning in." She stretched her arms. "I'll see you in the morning."

"Get your rest." Meggie wiped the table with the dish rag. "You want to enjoy the tour tomorrow."

Shirley halted in the middle of the front room and twisted around. "Meggie?"

Meggie raised her head and stopped wiping the table.

"You don't suppose . . . Robert the . . ."

"No, I don't suppose Robert the Doll had anything to do with the murder, so don't even go there."

"You're right. I didn't want to go there anyway."

Meggie finished cleaning and made a glass of iced tea. She made sure the doors were locked and turned the lights off. Upstairs she switched on the bedside lamp, opened the French door and walked onto the deck. The temperature hovered around seventy degrees and moonlight spilled across the yard. Overhead a jet plane broke the silence. She set her glass of iced tea on the small table next to the reclining chair and sat down. After adjusting the backrest she looked up at the moon. No matter what happened, she intended to enjoy the rest of her vacation.

CHAPTER 12

A WEEK LATER MEGGIE FELT QUEASY, turned over in bed and felt her stomach flip-flop. She sat up and then lay back down. Getting sick on vacation was not on her agenda, but murder had not been on her agenda either. She heard footsteps downstairs and glanced at the clock on the nightstand.

"Meggie!" Shirley called from below. "Are you up yet? It's 9:30."

Meggie pushed herself up and hung her knees over the bed. "I'm coming down now," she called. She rested one foot on the floor and tried to stand. Her head spun so she waited out the dizziness. When it passed, she padded to the stairway, gripped the hand railing and took the stairs one at a time. Meggie sat down on the couch and laid her head back.

Shirley bustled into the room. A green apron hung over her shoulders and her purple clothing peeked out from underneath. "What's your problem?"

"I'm not sure. I feel a little woozy and my eyes sting."

"Can I do something for you?" Shirley looked concerned. "Can I fix you a slice of dry toast and a cup of tea?"

Meggie fluffed the pillow, stretched out on the couch and closed her eyes. "A cup of tea would taste good."

"I'll make toast, too." Shirley hurried into the kitchen and a few minutes later returned with a cup of tea and a slice of dry toast. She set them on the coffee table. "There you go. I hope this does the trick."

"Thanks." Meggie sat up and sipped her tea.

"As much as I hate to say this," Shirley remarked, "I'd rather see you snooping than sick."

Meggie smiled and took a bite of toast. "Have you been outside yet?"

"It's hot and supposed to get hotter." Shirley untied her apron and took it off. "I don't care how hot it gets as long as we don't have a hurricane."

"There aren't any hurricanes in the forecast so I think we're safe." Shirley sat down on the end of the couch.

"If you want to do something today, go ahead." Meggie nibbled on her toast. "Don't sit and wait for me."

"If you're sure you don't mind staying alone, I might go for a bike ride." Shirley stretched her legs. "And hit some shops along Duvall Street."

"That sounds like fun," Meggie said, hoping it would take Shirley's mind off the murder.

"I'll have my phone with me." Shirley pushed herself off the couch. "If you need anything just call and I'll come home."

"Don't get lost." Meggie brushed a strand of hair off her face. "Call if you do."

"Yes, Mother." Shirley smiled. "I'll do that."

Meggie finished her tea and set the cup on the coffee table. She lay back, closed her eyes and fell asleep.

Mid-afternoon the front door slammed and Meggie bolted upright. Her heart hammered against her chest.

Shirley threw her backpack on the floor and tossed the shopping bag next to it. She pinched her lips. "I've never in my whole entire life seen anything like it."

Meggie shifted her position and rubbed her forehead. "What are you talking about?" She glanced at Shirley's shopping bag. "You made it to Duvall Street, I take it. You didn't get lost, did you?"

Shirley wiped her forehead with the palm of her hand and plopped down on the easy chair. Her hair clung to her neck. "I found Duvall Street all right. And a whole lot more than I expected."

"Tell me what happened." Meggie stretched her legs, lifted them onto the footstool and prepared herself for a long story.

Shirley licked her lips. "I'm walking along Duvall Street enjoying the day. MMOB."

Meggie smiled and tried to imagine Shirley minding her own business.

"You can see I did some shopping." Shirley nodded at the bag on the floor. "I ran into a few good deals and that panhandler wasn't around to bother me."

"I can see that," Meggie said.

"Anyway, I decide to stop for a beer." Shirley paused dramatically. "I see this open bar called the Bull and Whistle so I walk in and climb onto the bar stool. I hear this couple next to me talking about the Garden of Eden and we strike up a conversation."

"The Garden of Eden." A thought niggled at the back of Meggie's mind.

"You know how much I like gardens," Shirley said. "So I asked them for the address of the Garden of Eden." She sat forward in her chair. "I told them my friend had the most beautiful flower garden back in Minnesota."

"And that friend is me?" Meggie smiled.

Shirley nodded. "They gave me a strange look but at the time I didn't understand why."

"Did they give you the address of the garden?"

"They didn't have to. The man just pointed up and told me I was sitting under it."

"Sitting under it?"

"The Garden of Eden was on the rooftop of the Bull and Whistle Bar," Shirley said. "You can guess how excited I felt when I found out I was steps away from what sounded like a fine rooftop garden." Shirley threw her shoulders back. "So I finished my beer and walked out the way I came in. The man at the bar yelled something to me but I couldn't hear what he said."

"What did you do then?"

"I waved to them and climbed the stairs to the Garden of Eden. Let me tell you this." Shirley slapped her knee. "Did I ever have a shock."

"No garden?"

Shirley shook her head. "I'll say there was no garden. But I'll tell you what there was." She paused. "An old geezer standing by the bar, buck naked!"

Meggie threw her head back and burst out laughing. She recalled what Walter had told her about the Garden of Eden. "Shirley, that's a clothes optional bar."

"You certainly could have told me that." Shirley rose out of the easy chair and crossed her arms. "It would have saved me the humiliation and embarrassment of finding out for myself."

AFTER SHIRLEY'S EXPERIENCE in the Garden of Eden, the days in Key West sped by. Brian arrived to watch over the house until his mother and David returned. Meggie and Shirley boarded a plane for home. The black cloud that had descended after Ronald's murder lifted, but it hovered overhead all the way to Minnesota.

CHAPTER 13

W ALTER POURED COFFEE in his favorite mug. "We didn't bag many birds, but we had one heck of a good time."

"That's what matters." Meggie smiled. "Maybe you'll bag your limit next time."

Walter carried his coffee to the table and sat down. "It sure felt good to cross that hunting trip off my bucket list." He puffed out his chest and leaned back in the chair.

Meggie thought about the bucket list and how it seemed to give Walter a new lease on life. She noticed a spring in his step and a certain zest she hadn't seen for years.

The phone rang and interrupted her thoughts.

Walter pushed his chair back. "I'll get it." He strode to the counter and picked up the portable phone. "Sure thing." He handed it to Meggie and sat back down.

"Hi, Stella," Meggie said, smiling. "No, we're just finishing breakfast." Her smile disappeared. "Did you find out who it was?" She carried her coffee cup to the range and refilled it. "Sure . . . I'll call you back in a few minutes." Meggie laid the phone on the table in front of her.

"That was quick." Walter shoved a piece of bagel into his mouth. "What's the matter?"

Meggie took a deep breath. "Someone broke into Stella and David's cottage."

"Did they catch the guy?"

"Not yet." Meggie gazed out the window. "But I'll bet a dollar to a donut hole it has something to do with Ronald's murder."

"Too bad you're not in Key West." Walter stood and ruffled Meggie's hair. "You could do some investigating."

"It makes your day, doesn't it?"

Walter looked dazed. "I'm sure I don't know what you mean."

Meggie picked up her breakfast dishes. "I'm here in Pine Lake, Minnesota, too far away to get involved in any investigation."

Walter leaned against the counter and watched Meggie load the dishwasher.

"Stella isn't sure when they broke in," Meggie said.

Walter arched an eyebrow. "What?"

"She said they probably wouldn't have known about the break-in if they hadn't discovered the broken lock."

"How so?" Walter slapped his camo hunting cap on his head.

"There wasn't much left to steal inside the cottage." Meggie wiped the counter. "Stella thoroughly cleaned it when she returned from her cruise. She called Ronald's grandfather to see what she should do with everything. He suggested giving anything valuable to Ronald's cousin and to use her judgment on the rest of it."

"Wonder what they were looking for?"

"That," Meggie said, "is a good question."

"What do the police say?"

"Not much. They still have the case open but as far as Stella knows they have no leads."

"They'll catch the culprit—sooner or later," Walter said.

Meggie stared out the kitchen window and thought about Ronald. "This time I'll take Shirley's advice."

"What's that?"

"I plan to MMOB."

Walter tilted his head. "Say what?"

"Mind my own business."

Walter laughed and chucked her under the chin. "You don't really have a choice, do you?"

CHAPTER 14

OCTOBER HAD GOTTEN OFF to a cold start. Meggie shivered, threw back the covers and slipped on her robe. On the way to the kitchen she turned up the thermostat, thought about Indian summers and the possibility they might still enjoy one.

Meggie turned the burner on under the coffee and sat down at the computer. She opened an email from Stella and scanned the message. Her friend reported the police were no closer to solving Ronald's murder but the case was still open. Stella said everything had returned to normal for them and they still talked about how much they enjoyed the cruise.

"You're up early." Walter pulled on his robe and looked at the clock. "The paper should be here by now." He switched on the yard light and opened the front door.

Meggie finished reading Stella's email and shot off a reply. She stretched, walked to the counter and poured two cups of coffee. She set Walter's cup on the table.

"Brrr. It's starting to feel like old man winter." A blast of cold air followed Walter into the house.

"What do you want for breakfast?" Meggie asked.

"Toast and juice should do it."

"Wheat?"

"Uh-huh."

Meggie dropped two slices of bread in the toaster and set the orange juice on the table. "I received an email from Stella."

Walter sat down and opened the paper. "What's new with them?

Meggie cupped her coffee mug and leaned against the counter. "Good news. They're planning a trip to Minnesota in January."

Walter's lips turned up at the corners. "That is good news. In time for the fishing contest, I hope."

Meggie buttered Walter's toast, set it on a plate and handed it to him.

Walter spread raspberry jam on top of the melted butter. A guilty look spread across his face and he peeked up at Meggie. "A little jam isn't going to hurt anything."

Meggie bit her tongue. She didn't want to hassle Walter about what he should or shouldn't eat. "They plan to visit Brian in St. Paul, then head north to Pine Lake."

Walter took a bite of toast. "I'm glad they're coming here. It'll be something to look forward to." A hunk of raspberry jam hung from the corner of his mouth. "I just hope the fish are biting." He refilled his orange juice. "What time do you want to leave for the casino today?"

Meggie put a finger to her lip. "Let me think a minute. I'll call Shirley and see what time they're heading out."

Walter smirked. "I don't want to go that early."

"Be nice and don't pick on Shirley," Meggie said. "I'd like to get there by check-in time if that's all right with you."

"Sounds good." Walter pushed his chair back. "Are you going in to the shop today?"

"For a bit," Meggie said. "Vera has a doctor's appointment so I told her I'd cover." Vera kept the shop open during the fall and winter months but shortened the hours. Business fell after Labor Day and there weren't as many people in town. Pine Lake did see its share of ice fishing enthusiasts and snowmobilers but they didn't have a big effect on Hearts and Flowers Gift Shop.

Before Meggie left the house, she picked up the phone and punched in Shirley's number.

"Hello."

"Just wondering what time you and Bill are heading out to the casino."

"Bill wants to leave as late as possible." Shirley lowered her voice. "He says the later we leave the richer he'll be."

"He wants to go, right?" Meggie knew he liked blackjack but he felt the same way Walter did about the casino.

"He wants to go but he just won't admit it." Shirley laughed. "For some strange reason he thinks if he acts too interested I'll spend more money." She paused. "Men . . . go figure."

CHAPTER 15

MEGGIE ENJOYED THE DRIVE to the casino. The trip gave her a chance to relax and converse with Walter. They made good time and within the hour Walter pulled into the hotel parking lot. He took the keys out of the ignition and the luggage out of the trunk.

After they checked in, they went up to their room. Walter plopped down on the bed and turned the television on. "I wonder what channels they get here?" he said.

She shook her head and went into the bathroom to freshen up. When she came out, Walter had his feet propped up on a foot stool in front of the easy chair and his eyes glued to the television screen. "While you're doing that, I'm going downstairs."

Walter smiled. "Some machine calling your name, or what?"

Meggie ignored his little dig but wanted to suggest he attach a small television to his hip pocket and come along. "Meet you in front of the Grill around 5:30, okay?"

"Sure," Walter said. "It might cut into my news time but I'll be there."

Meggie cleared her throat and gave him an icy look.

"I'm just giving you a hard time." Walter laughed. "Don't spend all your money before dinner."

Meggie stepped off the elevator and heard the *ding ding* of the machines. She followed the sound through the brightly lit lobby into the darker gambling area. After helping herself to a complimentary cup of coffee, she lingered in the first aisle. She moved on and sat down at a machine near the blackjack table. She took out a five-dollar bill and fed it into the penny machine.

The machine cooled off after thirty minutes and Meggie checked her watch. She realized she had almost an hour before meeting the others. She prepared to leave and noticed a dealer step up to the blackjack table. He looked vaguely familiar but she couldn't place him. A machine tinged behind her and caught her attention. She peeked over the winner's shoulder and watched the credits rack up. Some people had all the luck.

Meggie stopped at several machines on her way to the Grill and dropped a couple bills in each of them. She neared the restaurant and glimpsed Walter, Bill and Shirley at the end of the waiting line. Walter turned, spotted her and poked Shirley.

"Did you spend all your money?" Shirley whispered.

Meggie shook her head. "I'm almost fifteen dollars ahead."

During dinner Walter and Bill discussed deer hunting while the women talked about the upcoming Halloween party the Legion Auxiliary planned to sponsor. After dinner the men headed to the blackjack tables and Shirley sat down at a nickel machine near the entrance to the Grill.

Meggie wandered the casino floor until she grew tired and decided to go up to her room. She found Walter at the blackjack table, tapped him on the shoulder and told him her plans to call it a night.

His eyes didn't leave the cards. "Catch you later."

On her way up to the room, Meggie figured out her losses and let her mind drift to the young blackjack dealer she had seen earlier in the evening. It irritated her when she couldn't put a name to a face but she knew sooner or later she would recall why he looked familiar.

Meggie didn't wait up for Walter and in a few minutes her eyes grew heavy and she dropped off to sleep.

"Up and at 'em, Meg."

Meggie's eyes opened halfway and focused on Walter.

He hovered over the bed, bent down and shook her shoulder a second time. "Time to rise and shine, Meggie-girl."

Meggie sat up and tried to open her eyes all the way.

Walter clapped her on the shoulder. "That's my girl."

She squinted at him. "What time is it?"

"Early." Walter looked at the bedside clock. "Almost eight."

Meggie hadn't seen Walter this pumped up since he made out his bucket list.

"What do you say we go down to the Grill for breakfast?" Walter asked.

"You're sure in a chipper mood this morning." She ran her fingers through her messed hair. "You win last night or something?"

Walter threw his shoulders back. He blew on his knuckles and rubbed them against his chest. "$200."

Meggie stuck her tongue out. She didn't mind him winning but she minded his rub-it-in-your-face attitude.

He shook his finger at her. "Now, now, little woman, don't be a poor loser." He kissed her on the forehead. "Breakfast is on me."

Meggie smiled at Walter. She planned to order the most expensive item on the menu.

CHAPTER 16

A FEW DAYS LATER MEGGIE picked up the phone and punched in Shirley's number. "Hi, Bill. Is Shirley around?"

"Yup."

Meggie heard Bill lay the phone down.

"Hang it up," Shirley yelled. "I have it up here."

Meggie heard a click and then Shirley came on the line.

"Am I catching you at a bad time?"

"Naw. Bill's driving me crazy, that's all."

Meggie laughed. "What's the poor guy done this time?"

"Poor guy?" Shirley lowered her voice. "He's gone into hunting mode . . . early."

"Uh-oh."

"He's been in the basement all week lining up his hunting gear," Shirley said. "And get this: he already started growing his beard."

"You know men and hunting, they're all alike."

"Hunting this and hunting that. I told Bill I don't want to croak during hunting season because he'd keep me in cold storage until it was over."

"Hey," Meggie said. "Not to change the subject, but I finally got around to printing some hard copies of the pictures I took in Key West."

"How did they turn out?"

"Great, but there's something interesting about one of them I'd like you to see," Meggie said.

"Interesting good or interesting bad?" Shirley asked.

"Do you want to meet me for lunch and I'll show you?"

"When and where?"

Meggie looked at her calendar. "You busy tomorrow? Say, noon at Pine Lake Café?"

THE NEXT DAY MEGGIE PULLED up in front of Pine Lake Café but didn't see Shirley's Taurus on the street. Before she could open the café door, Shirley pushed it open from the inside. "How's this for timing?"

"You're not late. Wonders never cease."

There were few customers inside the café so Shirley and Meggie had their choice of seats. They took a booth near the front of the restaurant and opened the menus.

Belle approached the booth and set two glasses of water in front of them. "Hannah had to run to the drug store so I'm cook and server for the time being."

Meggie had known Hannah, and her brother and sister since they were little. A single mom now, Hannah worked for her mother at the café.

Belle wiggled the pencil in her hand. "You gals need more time to decide?"

Meggie shook her head. "We're ready."

After Belle took their order and left, Shirley leaned over the table and held her hand out. "Let's see that picture."

Meggie opened her purse, took out an envelope and handed the picture to Shirley.

Shirley placed her readers on her nose and held the picture up. "Looks like a good picture to me." She glanced at Meggie. "What's the big deal about it?"

"Look again."

"You and me smiling at the camera." Shirley scrutinized it. "Me looking rotund. You looking too darn good for your age." She handed it back to Meggie. "Other than that it's a good picture."

Meggie held the photograph in front of Shirley and tapped it with her finger. "Who's this?"

"Ahh . . . that homeless guy we saw a hundred times." Shirley tilted her head. "He spoils the picture, doesn't he?" She looked at Meggie. "I give. Tell me what you're thinking."

"Remember the blackjack dealer I pointed out at the casino the other night? Don't you think he looks like the man in the picture?"

"Meggie," Shirley said. "Do you mean to tell me that's what this lunch is about?"

"There's something else." Meggie handed the picture back to Shirley. "Look at what he's wearing on his head."

"He has a red bandana wrapped around his head and . . . a chain around his neck." Shirley wrinkled her nose and gave the picture to Meggie. "He's grubby-looking."

Meggie reminded Shirley that a red bandana had been found near the pool the morning Ronald's body was discovered.

Shirley narrowed her eyes. "You think that homeless man murdered Ronald?"

"I don't know what I think." Meggie put the picture away. "I scanned the picture to Stella."

"Why?"

"I wanted to know if the panhandler was still down there."

"And?"

Meggie lifted her brows. "She hasn't seen him."

Shirley shook her head. "Doesn't prove a thing, Sherlock."

"My vibes tell me there's more than a coincidence going on here. The panhandler looks like a blackjack dealer in Minnesota and he wears a red bandana, the same color as the one found beside the pool. My vibes have kicked into alert mode."

CHAPTER 17

FOR THE MOST PART, Bluff is a sleepy little town that lives in the shadow of Pine Lake. On a good day the population is 351, but on the Saturday after Thanksgiving the population soars when the Fish House Parade comes to town.

Fish houses decorated wild and crazy are loaded onto trailers or hoisted onto the back end of pick-up trucks. They're paraded down Main Street in a celebration of winter and ice fishing. Businesses as well as private individuals enter and compete for prizes.

"Bill plans to enter the Fish House parade this year," Shirley announced to Meggie and Audrey over coffee at Swenson's bakery.

"You're kidding," Meggie said. "I thought he lost interest after he lost first place to Millie Munson two years ago."

Shirley pushed her chair back, walked to the counter and re-filled her coffee cup. "He changed his mind when I told him that was ancient history and he was being a poor sport."

"Why so glum, then?" Audrey asked.

"I didn't actually think he'd listen to me and change his mind." Shirley forced a laugh and sat down. "And that's not the worst part."

"Here we go." Meggie's lip turned up at the corners.

Shirley cleared her throat. "He expects me to ride on the float while he pulls it."

Meggie set her coffee down and broke her cranberry-orange muffin in half. "Come on, it sounds like fun. And we'll be there to cheer you on, won't we, Audrey?"

Audrey nodded. "Thomas and I plan to go and we'll give you moral support."

Shirley made eye contact with Meggie then Audrey. "I suppose in the end I'll have to do it, but that doesn't mean I'm going to like it."

CHAPTER 18

M EGGIE PULLED HER COAT ON, reached into the pocket and took out the handmade woolen mittens she had purchased at Hearts and Flowers.

Walter grabbed his winter jacket from the entryway closet and zipped it up. "Did you remember long johns?" He pulled his stocking cap over his head and opened the door.

"Yes, and extra jogging pants." Meggie stepped out in the cold and stopped by the outdoor thermometer on the side of the garage. She watched Walter plod toward the truck in his Sorel boots. "It's really rather mild," she called. "I just hope it doesn't go below freezing."

Meggie opened the passenger door, raised her foot and set it on the running board. She took hold of the grab handle and pulled herself up. Warm air blew in her face as she strapped her seat belt on. "The automatic starter sure is nice, huh?"

"One of the best Christmas presents I ever received, Santa." Walter's eyes crinkled. "What time does everything start today?" he asked.

"The parade begins at 1:00 p.m."

Walter twisted his head and backed around. "Why are we leaving so early?"

"I want to check out the craft items and baked goods before the parade." Meggie slipped off her mittens. "Besides, it's a hassle finding a parking space if you don't get there early."

"You're probably right," Walter murmured. "As usual."

"We can have lunch at the Legion, and don't forget there's live music." Meggie tickled Walter's chin. "It'll be fun."

"Hot drinks are half-price at the Legion, too." Walter turned on the radio. "That should help keep us warm."

Meggie knew the American Legion Post 49 in Bluff counted on the Fish House Parade to bring in money. She knew, too, Walter looked forward to half-price drinks. "I'll be the designated driver today," Meggie said.

"Do you think Audrey and Thomas will show?" Walter asked and turned down the radio.

"As far as I know." Meggie chuckled.

"What's so funny?"

"I was just thinking about Shirley and her matchmaking."

"I hear ya." Walter grumbled. "She finally succeeded."

The side roads near Bluff were lined with vehicles when they arrived. Walter drove past the watertower and turned left onto Main Street. He took a left off Main Street and slid into an empty slot a half-block down River Street.

Meggie crawled out of the truck and helped Walter unload the camp chairs. She followed him through a small parking lot and onto Main Street. She scanned the area and located Audrey and Thomas sitting in front of Darla's Hair Fashions. They had their heads together and were sharing something funny. Meggie and Walter plodded across the street.

Audrey lifted her hand in acknowledgment when she saw them.

"Thanks for saving us a spot." Meggie opened her camp chair and set it next to Audrey.

"I hear we're going to have quite the show today." Walter sat down next to Meggie and looked around.

After a couple minutes of chit-chat Meggie stood. "Now that we have our spots, does anyone feel like looking around?"

"I'd like to look at the crafts," Audrey said.

"You men want to join us?" Meggie asked.

Walter grinned. "I'd like to check out the fishing tackle at the hardware booth."

"I think I'll join you, Walt." Thomas folded his blanket. "Do you think we'll have our spots and chairs if we all leave?"

Walter shrugged. "Not much chance anyone will take them."

Meggie and Audrey excused themselves and walked around the corner to the Legion Club. Meggie opened the door and stepped into a large room next to the bar area. Tables filled with crafts lined the walls and ran down the center of the room. Laughter mingled with loud conversation. Boots clomped and children shrieked. A large crowd mulled around.

"Oh, look." Audrey held up a pair of rabbit fur mittens. "Don't these look warm?" She picked up a matching hat. "I think I'll buy them for Thomas."

"He'll like those," Meggie said. "I think I'll meander." She walked past several tables displaying Christmas items—sparkly ornaments, Christmas towels and homemade Christmas greeting cards. She occasionally paused to check out an item or two. After making the rounds, she returned to the first table and purchased a box of Christmas cards. She waited for Audrey near the door.

Belle Fossen burst into the craft room from outside. "Hello, Meggie."

"You must be taking the day off."

"Yup." Belle lowered her voice. "Kenny insisted on being in the parade and I told him if he could play I could, too." She stepped away and called over her shoulder. "The kids are holding down the fort."

A blast of cold air hit Meggie and she turned around. Walter and Thomas strode through the door empty-handed.

"No fishing tackle?"

Walter shook his head and wiped the fog off his glasses. "None that I wanted or needed. You ready to eat?"

Thomas slapped his gloved hands together and spotted Audrey at a nearby craft table. "Save us a place," he said.

WALTER SURVEYED THE BAR area and nodded toward a table. "How about over there?"

Meggie pulled out a chair and sat down.

A waitress approached their table. "What can I get you folks?"

"Coffee for me and menus, please." Meggie smiled up at the young girl.

"I'll have a hot buttered rum," Walter said and slipped his jacket off. "It gets a little nippy out there."

"Well, I'll be." A voice boomed from the bar.

Meggie looked up.

"Never know what the cat's gonna drag in." Bud Anderson, grizzled and hairy, climbed off the bar stool and ambled toward them.

Walter stood, grabbed hold of Bud's hand and pumped it up and down. "How are you doing, Bud? Have a chair."

Bud's gray beard rested against a faded red-and-black checkered flannel shirt with a tiny hole near the pocket. He set his bottle of beer on the table and pulled up the suspenders on his pants. "Hello, Meggie." He held out his hand and smiled.

She took his hand and wondered how he was doing since the death of his grand-nephew. "How are you, Bud? I haven't seen you for a while."

Walter grabbed two chairs from a nearby table when Audrey and Thomas approached them. He motioned them to sit down. "I'd like you to meet Bud Anderson, a friend of my family." Walter turned toward Bud. "These are friends of ours, Audrey Peterson and Thomas Murphy."

Bud stood and extended his hand. "Pleased to meetcha."

The waitress set Meggie and Walter's drinks on the table and handed them menus. She turned to Audrey and Thomas and took their orders, then turned to go.

"Hey, good lookin'."

The waitress turned back and smiled at Bud.

He held up his empty bottle and winked. "I'll have me another."

The young girl blushed and told him she would be right back with his beer.

Bud spoke to Audrey and Thomas and nodded at Walter. "I knew your friend here when he was knee-high to a grasshopper. He was just a little tyke."

Walter grinned and sipped his buttered rum.

"His ma and pa were friends of mine, neighbors."

"Where do you live, Bud?" Thomas asked.

"I have 160 acres north of town. Not too far from here."

"It's a beautiful area," Walter said. "My folks chose a good place to raise a bunch of kids when they bought that land next to you."

Bud told them about the forty acres he gave his grand-nephew a couple years earlier. "I shouldn't-a done it." He took a long swallow of beer. "Poor Ronnie."

"Did you get the land back?" Walter tapped his mug.

Bud looked down at the table. "Ronnie sold it off to a couple guys he met in St. Paul." He paused. "I told him he could do what he wanted with it." Bud slapped his knee and pushed his chair back. "I best leave before my stool at the bar cools off." He laid his hand on Walter's shoulder. "You come into Bluff some night and play bar bingo here at the Legion."

"I'll do that."

Bud saluted and ambled back to the bar.

"He's a great old guy." Walter's eyes misted. "He's been around Bluff forever."

"He seems very nice," Audrey said. "Does he live alone?"

Walter nodded. "Yes. He lost his wife and children years ago in a car accident."

CHAPTER 19

SPECTATORS CROWDED THE SIDEWALK on both sides of Main Street. Folks stood, sat in chairs or moved to keep warm. Children pranced and gripped their empty candy bags. Loud music played over a loud speaker from the judge's platform.

"Almost 1:30." Walter's breath clouded. "Parade should be here by now."

Meggie slipped her readers on and read the parade route flyer. "They're lining up at Bluff City Park." She looked at Walter.

"I'm listening." He slapped his hands together and stomped his feet.

"The parade will follow Blueberry River for a short distance and then wind its way toward Main Street."

"Does anyone know Bill's parade number?" Thomas asked.

"Shirley wouldn't tell us," Meggie said. "She wanted to keep everything hush-hush."

Audrey leaned toward Meggie. "Shirley wouldn't even tell me how they were decorating the fish house."

A siren wailed in the distance.

"They're coming," Audrey said.

Meggie stood on tiptoe and craned her neck.

A police car turned onto Main Street and two firetrucks clanged behind it. Bluff's mayor and grand marshal, Ernest Fisk, waved from a horse-drawn carriage, and Santa Claus and Mrs. Claus tossed candy from a candy-striped float. Children squealed and scurried into the street. They snatched at the candy and ran back to the curb.

"Here come the houses," Walter said.

"I can't wait to see how Bill decorated his fish house." Audrey stepped closer to the curb.

"Look. There's Bill's truck." Meggie pulled Walter to the curb.

"What the heck? It looks like he's pulling an outhouse." Walter waved.

"Oh, my gosh," Meggie laughed.

Walter cupped his mouth. "That your portable potty, Wright?"

Bill raised a clenched fist, slowed down and idled the truck in front of them.

"Where's the missus?" Walter shouted.

The truck jerked forward. Meggie couldn't see Shirley but noticed the door at the back of the fish house hung open. The float passed in front of her. Shirley, dressed in long johns and a warm hat with fur-trimmed ear flaps, sat on the john. She held a fishing pole in one hand, a can of beer in the other.

Audrey's shoulders shook. She twisted her neck and leaned close to Meggie. "I can't let Shirley see me laugh."

"You think she's enjoying the ride?" Walter chuckled.

Meggie shook her head. "I don't think so."

After the parade was over, Meggie noticed Bud in the crosswalk on the side street in front of the Legion. A silver truck idled in front of him. Bud waved his arms around and pointed his finger at the driver. The driver shouted at him and drove into the intersection. Meggie couldn't hear what the driver said but she knew it wasn't Minnesota nice.

CHAPTER 20

"THEY SHOULD BE GETTING HERE SOON." Walter sat down on his recliner and glanced at the clock above the bay window. He flipped through the channels and selected the WCCO News report.

Meggie turned the temperature down and closed the oven door. "We'll keep their supper warm until they get here." She carried a cup of tea into the front room.

"Another meth house busted." Walter stretched out on the recliner. "This time it's near Hibbing."

A picture of the house flashed on the screen. "It looks like it's out in the sticks," Meggie said. "Children lived there, too. What a shame."

"Yup. It sure is." Walter patted the arm of the chair. "I worry about Bud out in the boondocks by himself." He glanced at Meggie. "I didn't want to mention it, but someone busted his front window."

"What? Did he report it?" She didn't like the idea of Bud living in the country, either.

"I took care of it." The weather report came on and Walter turned the volume up. "Looks like this cold spell is gonna break."

Meggie needed relief from the below-zero temperatures Pine Lake had been experiencing for the past two weeks. "I hope it breaks tonight in time for the fishing contest tomorrow."

Of his two visits to Minnesota since he married Stella, David had told Meggie and Walter he enjoyed the winter vacation most and promised them his next trip would be in time for the Pine Lake Lions' fishing contest.

"What time did they leave Brian's?" Walter crossed his arms under the back of his neck.

Two headlights turned into the driveway. "I think they're here." Meggie walked to the front door and switched on the yard light.

Walter pushed himself up from the recliner, walked to the closet and slipped on his parka. "I'll help them with the luggage."

Meggie waited by the storm door, cleared a small area of ice with her sleeve and peeked through. She saw Stella crawl out of the car. Walter said something and his breath fogged. Stella laughed, clutched her arms and hurried up the walk.

Meggie opened the door and stepped aside. "Come on in."

"It's cold out there." Stella gave Meggie a hug.

"Let me take your coat," Meggie said. She hung it in the entryway closet and led Stella to the kitchen. "Would you like some coffee or tea?"

"I'd love some. Whatever's convenient."

Meggie set the tea diffuser in the green teapot and poured hot water over it. "I have your supper ready if you're hungry."

The front door slammed. David and Walter carried the luggage into the house and set it down by the door. They shed their coats and joined Meggie and Stella in the kitchen.

"Greetings, David." Meggie gave him a hug. "I hope you brought your appetite."

DAVID SLID HIS PLATE AWAY and rubbed his stomach. "That wild rice hot dish sure hit the spot."

"We'll take some wild rice home with us," Stella said. "I'll need your recipe, Meggie."

The four friends talked at the table, then moved into the front room.

"It's good to be back in Minnesota," David said.

"You're always welcome, you know." Walter picked up Peppie. "I just hope you're not disappointed if the fish don't bite."

"Believe me, he doesn't care if they bite or not." Stella touched David's knee. "He's into this whole rugged outdoor he-man scene."

David laughed.

Meggie chimed in. "I remember my mother told me if I married a Minnesotan, I better like to hunt and fish."

"And if you marry a hunter or fisherman and don't like to hunt and fish," Walter added, "you'll end up a hunting widow."

Meggie grimaced. "You got that right."

Later, Meggie showed Stella to the guest room.

"What time does the contest start in the morning?" Stella asked.

"The contest doesn't start until ten but we need to get there early to get good fishing holes." Meggie paused. "I'll check with Walter, but we should leave the house by eight or eight thirty. We'll want to look over the prizes and buy raffle tickets before the contest starts."

"Something tells me that tomorrow is going to be a long day."

"It will be long and unless this weather changes, mighty cold."

The next morning cars and trucks were lined up on both sides of the road near the entrance to the fishing contest.

"Looks like a good turnout today," David remarked.

"Yup." Walter parked behind a green, dented pickup. "That looks like Bud Anderson's truck."

Meggie hadn't seen Bud since the Fish House parade. Walter said he didn't leave the house very often and she wondered if it had anything to do with the vandalism.

"Bud Anderson?" Stella asked.

Meggie sat in the small side seat behind the others. "We told him you were visiting."

"I hope he's doing all right." Stella sounded concerned.

"Everybody out." Walter pulled the keys from the ignition and crawled out of the truck." He opened the camper top, lowered the gate and pulled two plastic sleds out. He set them on the ground and crawled inside the back of the truck. "David," he said, "I'll hand you everything. Just set it on the sleds."

David reached for the portable folding chairs.

"Better set two on each sled in case we don't get four holes together. Here's the fishing bait," Walter said.

"Straight from the gas station."

"Around here minnows at the gas station are almost as important as the gas." Walter handed David the ice fishing poles. "I think we're all set." He crawled out of the truck and led them to four ice holes.

Walter had just finished rigging his line when Meggie heard someone call his name. Bud Anderson sauntered toward them. "Mind if I fish here with you?"

Walter clapped Bud on the back. "You don't have to ask. Look who we brought with us."

"Meggie. Stella." Bud tipped his hat and turned to David. "Don't believe I've met the hubbie."

David held out his hand and Bud shook it. "I want to thank you for being so good to Ronnie. He thought the world of you folks."

Meggie looked at her watch. "It's almost time." The whistle blew and the lines dropped down the holes.

Bud shuffled his feet to keep them warm. "I still think a lot about Ronnie." He looked away then back at David. "Are they still lookin' for leads down there?"

David nodded. "Sooner or later something will turn up."

"You have any idea why someone would want to kill my nephew?" Bud's voice cracked.

David shook his head.

"Ronald seemed distant for some time." Stella tugged on her line. "He told me once he regretted selling his land." She pulled the line out of the water, checked it and dropped it down in the hole. "The last time I spoke to him he had changed."

Meggie looked at Stella through the falling snow. "How so?" She took her hand out of her mitten and blew on her fingers.

"He told me he had plans to get the land back. He said it wouldn't be long and Uncle Bud would thank him."

Bud lowered his head. "I've been havin' trouble at the home place." He tipped his winter cap back and scratched his head. "I wonder if it ain't those yahoos that bought the land from Ronnie that's givin' me trouble."

"That wind is picking up," Walter said and pulled his line out of the water. "Time's up in a minute anyway." The wind moaned and the snow swirled around them.

Meggie pulled her line up and realized she was hungry and thirsty.

"What do you say to lunch at the Legion?" Walter struggled to keep the fishing paraphernalia from sliding off his sled.

Meggie smiled to herself. *Great minds think alike . . . and so do fools.*

CHAPTER 21

S HIRLEY BACKED INTO THE FRONT SEAT of the Bug holding her hat
in place with her hand. She turned in the seat and faced the
windshield. "This car is too small for my hat." A red silk rose
drooped over the wide brim.

"Maybe your hat is too big for the Bug." Meggie's eyes grew
round and hinted mischief.

"That could be." Shirley buckled her seatbelt and smoothed her
red dress. "I hope Audrey isn't late. You know how I like to be on time."

Meggie put the car in gear and glanced in the sideview mirror.
"And that's why you're always late?" She pulled away from the curb.
"You know Audrey. She'll be on time."

Shirley shrugged. "I suppose you're right."

"You're worried, aren't you?" Meggie sniffed the spring air.

Shirley reached into her purse, took out a small bottle of spray
cologne and misted her neck.

Meggie wrinkled her nose. "That's strong." She waved her hand
in front of her face.

"Elizabeth Arden's 'Red Door.'" Shirley glanced at Meggie.
"Why should I be worried?"

"You're afraid Marjorie Winkman will get to the tea before you
do and grab our table."

"No way." Shirley shook her head back and forth. "It's true I
like that table by the buffet but I wouldn't try to beat Marjorie
Winkman to it." She pressed her lips together. "I'm a little above that
kind of behavior."

Meggie arched her brows as the corners of her mouth turned up.

"You know she comes earlier every year," Shirley murmured
and opened a tube of lipstick. "She does it just to beat me to that table."

Meggie slowed the Bug and turned right on Nelson Road. She pulled up in front of a small white house surrounded by a picket fence.

"See, I told you." Meggie pointed at the house. "There she is, ready and waiting."

Audrey stood in the window, waved, and dropped the curtain back into place.

"Here I go again." Shirley struggled to get out of the car. "Why didn't we take my Taurus?"

"Hi, everyone." Audrey gathered her white eyelet dress around herself and crawled into the back seat. "I didn't know if I'd need my shawl but I brought it along."

"Right on time, as usual," Shirley said. "I love your dress."

Audrey blushed. "Thank you."

"You look nice, Audie." Meggie met Audrey's eyes in the rearview mirror. "I still like your hat." She looked out the driver's window and made a U-turn.

"I do, too." Audrey giggled. "Even if it's the same pillbox hat I wear every year." She paused. "My mother loved this hat and wore it everywhere." Audrey cleared her throat. "I couldn't bear to part with it when she died."

"That hat has seen more Mother's Day Teas than I have." Shirley pushed the drooping rose onto the brim of her hat. "It's a good match for your pink shawl."

Meggie slowed the Bug and turned right into the parking lot at the Methodist church.

Shirley sat forward and craned her neck. "Thank heavens." She lifted the seat belt off. "I don't see that woman's car here yet."

"See, all that worrying for nothing." Meggie killed the engine. "Marjorie may not even show up today."

"She'll be here." Shirley helped Audrey out of the back seat. "I heard her yakking to Belle the other day at Pine Lake Café." Shirley turned up her nose. "She told Belle she bought a bright yellow dress for the occasion. I'm sure she plans to be the belle of the ball."

"Be nice, Shirley," Meggie said.

Shirley adjusted her hat and swept her arm towards the church hall entrance. "Shall we, ladies?"

Women in spring-colored dresses filed through the lobby. They greeted one another, laughed and giggled. An occasional titter erupted and hats in various colors and styles bobbed up and down.

Shirley fidgeted and peered around the lady in front of her. She held her hand to her mouth and whispered. "This line can start moving anytime now."

Lydia Erickson, Bud Anderson's sister, sat at the ticket table. A member of the Pine Lake Lions Club since its founding, she greeted the ladies as they passed by. Meggie signed her ticket, dropped it in the door prize basket and moved into the tea room. Sunlight danced through the tall windows and a floral scent tickled her nose.

Shirley hurried to the table next to the buffet table and signaled to Meggie and Audrey. "Isn't this nice?" She pulled out two chairs and motioned them to sit. "We've been transported to a delightful English garden." She laid her purse on a third chair, threw her shoulders back and pulled in her stomach. "I'm going to mingle."

Meggie watched Shirley scoot to the far side of the room and tap a tall lady on the shoulder. Meggie grinned at Audrey. "She's on her gossip mission."

"Shirley is one of a kind." Audrey picked up the program and glanced around the room. "They certainly have decorated nicely."

"I'm glad they chose the English Garden theme this year." Meggie noticed the microphone next to the buffet table. "I'm anxious to hear the program." She leaned forward and picked up the vase of cut flowers from the center of the table. She sniffed the miniature pink and white roses and purple carnations. "I love the smell of carnations." She fingered the baby's breath and set the vase down.

The off-white crocheted tablecloth Vera's cousin, Nettie, had donated several years earlier to the ladies church group covered the buffet table. A wooden trellis stood near the microphone and green vines trailed over the top and down the sides.

Meggie scanned the program. "Oh!" she exclaimed. "They're having rum cake."

"They served rum cake a few years ago." Audrey's eyes lit up. "It was the first time I tasted it and I loved it."

Meggie heard a racket behind her, glanced over her shoulder and observed Shirley trying to squeeze through two tables. She hurried towards them and leaned close to Meggie. "You can stop worrying now. Vera and Nettie just pulled in." She grabbed her purse off the chair and sat down. "Thank heavens."

"I'm relieved to hear that." Meggie turned to Audrey. "Vera didn't feel well yesterday and wasn't sure if she'd feel any better today." She lowered her voice. "I worry about Nettie's driving."

"That makes two of us." Shirley took her white gloves off and set them on the table.

"I expressed my concerns to Vera but she brushed them off," Meggie said.

"I tell you, the way that woman drives it's a wonder they're still alive." Shirley shook her head.

Vera and Nettie stood under the arched doorway and scanned the room. Nettie's eyes zeroed in on Meggie and she whispered to Vera. They both smiled and waved. Vera's lavender dress floated around her on the way to the table. She paused several times to greet friends. Nettie, plump and slightly taller than Vera, followed close behind. Her dark brown dress hung to the floor and matched the black-eyed Susans laced through her straw hat.

"Look at all of you," Nettie crooned and rubbed Meggie's shoulder. "You look so nice."

Meggie helped them get settled and admired Vera's bonnet decorated with sprigs of silk lilacs. "You two look like a breath of fresh air."

Shirley laid her gloves on the table. "Have any trouble on the road?"

Meggie glared at Shirley.

Audrey spoke up. "I don't know how you do it. You don't seem to age."

Nettie preened and smiled at Audrey. "Don't I wish."

Vera's eyes sparkled and she tapped Audrey's wrist. "If you find the fountain of youth, dear, don't drink it all."

Nettie tittered.

Women poured through the door and scurried to empty chairs.

Belle Fossen waved from the kitchen and Meggie wiggled her fingers in acknowledgment. Belle, a long-time Lion's member, made sure the buffet ran smoothly.

Women bustled in and out of the kitchen. They carried plates of tea sandwiches, scones and cookies, all donated from members of the club. They set them on the buffet table and returned to the kitchen for more. Only one empty spot remained on the table when Belle carried the rum cake from the kitchen. She set it down and scattered rose petals around it.

The president walked up to the microphone. "Ladies." Women continued to chatter. "Ladies." Several women tapped the side of their tea cups and a hush fell over the room. "Thank you all for coming out on such a beautiful spring day." The president spoke on the role the Pine Lake Lions played in the community and promised a delightful program to follow later. After the blessing, she instructed the table in the far corner of the room to start the buffet line.

"All right girls, who wants to pour tea this year?" Shirley glanced around the table.

Meggie raised her hand. "It's my turn. Audrey poured last year."

Later, after everyone at the table finished their rum cake, Meggie poured each of them a last cup of tea. She heard a *click-clack* behind her and turned around to see Lydia approach the table.

"Vera." Lydia bent down and gave Vera a hug. "I must have missed you at the ticket table."

"Lydia." Vera's face lit up. "How are you?"

"I'm doing fine." She rested her hand on the back of Vera's chair. "For someone my age." She tilted her head sideways and looked closely at Vera. "I don't need to ask how you are." Lydia winked at Meggie over Vera's head. "I've heard about the new man in your life."

Vera blushed, mumbled something about Eldon and changed the subject. "Lydia, do you remember Meggie?"

"Why, of course I do." She took Meggie's hand. "We didn't get a chance to talk earlier."

Meggie smiled. "I haven't seen you in ages."

"I remember we met some years back at Bud's house."

"Yes." Meggie sat back in her chair. "Walter introduced me to Bud for the first time that day." She turned to Audrey and Shirley and introduced them to Lydia.

"It's been a lovely day, but I do believe it's time to go home." Vera collected her purse and gloves.

Meggie noticed Audrey and Shirley were no longer sitting at the table. She pushed her chair back to leave.

"Grandma." A pretty young woman who looked to be in her late twenties touched Lydia's arm. "We should be going."

Lydia wrapped her arm around the young woman. "Vera Cunningham, I'd like you to meet my granddaughter, Beth Erickson."

Vera smiled and held out her hand. "You look just like your grandmother did when I first met her, hair like sunshine."

"Vera is an old friend of mine." Lydia grinned at Vera. "Please don't take 'old' the wrong way."

Vera giggled and let go of Beth's hand. "I wouldn't dream of it, since you and I are the same age." She nodded toward Meggie. "Beth, this is my friend and co-worker, Meggie Moore."

Beth met Meggie's eyes, murmured a greeting and looked away. She took a step back and said, "We should be going, Grandma."

"Lydia and Beth." Meggie lowered her voice. "I am so sorry about Ronald."

Lydia reached for Meggie's hand and squeezed it. "Thank you." Tears welled in her eyes. "It's been a difficult time for the family."

Beth cleared her throat and looked down at the floor.

"I understand you were housesitting at the time for Stella and David." Lydia paused. "I'm sure it was a trying time for you." She looked at Beth. "And for Beth as well."

"Grandma."

"Beth was living in Key West when Ronnie was murdered."

"Grandma, it's time to go." Beth took hold of her grandmother's arm.

"Yes, we should be on our way." Lydia hesitated and threw her shoulders back. "Ronald was a good child. He had a hard life. His mother died so young and he never knew his father." A tear rolled down her cheek. "I pray for the unfortunate boy daily."

CHAPTER 22

MORNING SUNLIGHT STREAMED across the bed and over Meggie. Her face tickled. She reached up to scratch it and felt something warm and hairy next to her. Her eyes opened and Peppie stuck his nose in her face. "Is it time for me to rise and shine, Peppie?" She slid off the bed and pulled the curtain aside. The weatherman had predicted a wet Monday but she couldn't see a cloud in the sky. It looked like another beautiful July day.

Meggie poured a cup of coffee and picked up a note from the counter. GOLFING WITH BILL. BACK WHEN I'M BACK. She scrunched it and tossed it into the garbage. The Carolina wren sang from the bird clock and Meggie shifted into high gear.

The week before, she ran into Bud Anderson at Swenson's Bakery and he invited her to pick blueberries on his property. He boasted several patches. "The bears don't need all the berries," he told her. She didn't like the idea of meeting up with a bear, but what were the chances? She picked up the phone and punched in Shirley's number.

"Hi. It's just me." Meggie cleared her throat. "You still up for picking blueberries this morning?"

"Yeah, I suppose." Shirley sighed.

"You don't sound too enthused."

"I love the berries but I'm not fond of picking them."

Meggie reminded Shirley of all the things she could do with the blueberries.

"And then I can spend the winter taking off the extra weight from all the blueberry goodies."

"It's going to be hot today so we need to get out there a.s.a.p." Meggie tapped the counter. "What time can you be ready?"

"I'm ready now. I couldn't sleep last night for some reason."

"You're tired," Meggie said. "That's all the more reason to beat feet. I'll pick you up between eight and eight thirty, and don't forget the hats."

"Not to worry. I'm looking at them as we speak."

Meggie pushed hangar after hangar aside in the closet. At the end of the rack she found a pair of long cotton pants and a long-sleeved lightweight shirt. She had picked enough blueberries during her lifetime to know it would be a miserable experience if she didn't dress for it. She made a mental note to grab her bug spray before she left the house.

Meggie stuffed a couple apples and several sticks of venison jerky in a lunch bag. She picked up the thermos of ice water and stowed it in the Bug's trunk next to the berry buckets and left to pick her friend up.

Shirley waited at the picnic table in front of her house with her berry picking paraphernalia on the table in front of her.

"Need some help?" Meggie called from the car.

Shirley shook her head, picked up her purse and slung it over her shoulder. In one hand she carried the berry buckets and in the other the straw hats.

Meggie jumped out of the car and opened the trunk. She pushed the water thermos to the back in order to make room for Shirley's gear.

"You're right on time." Shirley set her blueberry picking supplies in the trunk. "I hope we get enough berries to make it worth our while."

Meggie recalled the first time she picked blueberries at age ten. Her grandmother tried to talk her out of going and warned her about the bugs and the possibility of bears. Meggie said she didn't care about bugs or bears. She wanted to go blueberry picking and that was that.

"Did you bring your bell?" Meggie asked.

"That was the first thing I grabbed." Shirley smirked. "Let's just hope if we meet a bear, he isn't hard of hearing."

Meggie thought about the bell her grandmother made her wear.

"How does this look?" Shirley donned a straw hat. Netting hung from the brim and rested on her shoulders. "I don't think those deer flies will get past this."

"It looks bug proof. Let's just hope the bugs know that." Meggie gave Shirley credit for coming up with the idea.

Meggie turned left and drove through town past Hearts and Flowers Gift Shop. She spotted Eldon on the sidewalk near the shop and tooted the horn. He turned and waved to them.

The Bug clipped along Highway 52. "I love this time of year, don't you?" Meggie asked.

"It beats forty-below." Shirley wiped her brow. "I don't mind the heat so much but the humidity kills me."

"Roll your window up and I'll turn on the air," Meggie said.

The Bug ate up the twenty miles to Bluff in a short space of time. Meggie drove past St. James Catholic Church and First Lutheran Church on the right side of Main Street. A small independent gas station stood on the left side of the street next to Emma's Café and across the street from Lou's Bar.

"This must be the road," Meggie said. "First road to the left after Main Street, wasn't it?"

"It beats me. I've never been to Bud's." Shirley gazed around. "How far out does he live?"

"Three miles as the crow flies."

Shirley shot her a look.

"Bud's directions, not mine," Meggie said. "I haven't been out to his place in a while. Walter usually drives and I don't pay much attention to where he's going." Meggie hit the TRIP button on her odometer and the Bug bumped along the dirt road. She glimpsed a small yellow farmhouse nestled on a rolling hill to her left. Chickens ran free in the yard. Horses grazed and their tails swished from side to side. Several cows stood along the fence and two or three rested on the ground. Their eyes ogled them as they passed by.

Meggie drove close to a mile before the scenery changed. The fields were replaced by pines, birch and poplar trees. Two willow trees gracefully spread their branches over a small stream on the right side of the road.

"I see a fire number," Shirley said. "14467."

"That's it." Meggie turned the wheel and maneuvered the Bug up the long and narrow driveway. "Bud needs a big load of gravel on this road."

"I guess he does." Shirley gripped the door handle. "Maybe I'll bounce some weight off."

Meggie shifted into low, skirted a dip in the road and cranked the wheel to the right. "We have arrived."

CHAPTER 23

THE OLD FARMHOUSE SHOWED HER AGE, but proudly sported a fresh coat of paint. Meggie shut the Bug off and rested her eyes on a rusted Ford with no tires. It sat on the other side of a small garden and obviously had been parked there for some time. Bud's green, dented Chevy truck sat in front of the house.

The screen door flew open and Bud marched out. He wore suspender pants and a white t-shirt that looked like it had seen more than a few washings.

Meggie pushed her bangs away from her face and crawled out of the car. A crow cawed from a nearby tree. "We made it."

Bud climbed down the front steps and strode out to meet her. "Did ya have any trouble finding the place?"

"No trouble at all," Shirley said and stretched her arms.

"Well, young ladies," Bud pulled up his pants and looked at the sun. "Time is of the essence."

A red-headed woodpecker flew to a rotted pine tree near them and knocked its beak against the trunk. Bud waved his hand toward the noisy bird. "Never mind him. He makes a racket to get attention and to let me know he's around." Bud scratched his arm. "I best get you pickin' before it gets too hot."

Meggie and Shirley listened to Bud explain about the logging roads that ran through his property. He swept his arm in front of him and to the side. "I own 160 acres." He pointed beyond the driveway. "Over there are the forty acres I gave away."

"That's the land Ronald owned?" Meggie said.

"Yup." Bud pushed a sweat-stained cap up and scratched his head. "Now those crazy Williams boys own it." He looked at Meggie. "You'll know their land if you run into it. They got trespassing signs all over."

Meggie and Shirley looked at each other.

"Not sure what they have over there that's so durn valuable." His grin showed his missing tooth. "Maybe I'll just have to take me a walk one of these days and find out." He pointed to the ground. "You gals wait right here for me." He shuffled a couple steps and looked over his shoulder. "I keep my four-wheeler locked up tighter than a drum. Ya jist can't trust folks these days."

Meggie applied bug spray and handed it to Shirley. A low rumble came from the other side of the farmhouse and grew louder. The four-wheeler rolled around the corner of the house and Bud threw the brake less than a foot from the Bug. "Follow me in your car." He instructed them. "If it gets too rough, I'll put you in this here trailer."

Shirley glanced at the homemade trailer, then at Meggie. "Let's just hope the road doesn't get rough." She watched Bud back up and turn around. "I don't think I want to crawl into that old thing."

The Bug followed the four-wheeler out of the yard. "Why not?" Meggie steered the car onto the road leading to the woods and shifted into low. "It might be a fun adventure."

Shirley shrugged and leaned out the window. "I wonder how far we have to go into the woods."

Meggie knew they were handed an opportunity to pick blueberries on Bud's property. Locals normally kept locations of blueberry patches guarded secrets, but she and Shirley were invited to pick not one, but several patches.

Meggie took her eyes off the road for an instant and the Bug's right front tire hit a rut and bottomed out. She slid the car into reverse and pressed on the gas. Rocks scraped the bottom of the car. She tooted the horn to alert Bud, then shifted into neutral.

Bud pulled up alongside the car, bent his head down and peered in. "Need some help gettin' out?" He stretched his neck and looked the Bug over from one end to the other. "I think I could pick it up and move it myself if I had to." He threw his head back and laughed.

Meggie stuck her head out the window and turned her nose up at the fumes. "Should I give it more gas?"

Bud took his time getting off the four-wheeler. "Let me help ya." He walked around to the front of the vehicle. "Hey, little lady." He curled his finger at Shirley. "Give me a hand here."

Shirley got out of the car and joined him in front of the Bug.

"Shove 'er in reverse," Bud ordered. He bent down and said something to Shirley.

Shirley rolled her eyes and bent over next to Bud.

Meggie felt the front of the Bug raise slightly.

"Now give it gas," Bud shouted and pushed the Bug until it cleared the rut. He ambled to the driver's side. "There's a good patch just up ahead." Sweat ran down his face. "That might be a good place to start."

Meggie had no desire to drive any further than necessary. One patch was probably as good as another.

"Let's pick there," Shirley whispered. "If we go too far into the woods we have more chance of meeting up with bears."

"If you want," Bud suggested, "I can drive your car back and you can take the four-wheeler."

Meggie didn't like the idea of Bud driving her Bug and she didn't like the idea of driving the four-wheeler, either. "No, that's fine." She stroked her throat. "How is the road up ahead?"

"Not much better." Bud walloped his arm. "Durn flies." A deer fly lit on his nose and he pawed his face. "Maybe you best leave the car here."

Meggie bit her lip and looked at Shirley.

"I'll haul you up to the patch in the trailer. Think you can walk back to the car when you're done?" Bud took his cap off and mopped his head with his handkerchief. "I could come back and give you a ride if you'd rather."

Meggie hesitated. "How far is it to the patch?" She knew how vulnerable they would be without the car.

"Not far," he said. "'Course, it depends." He grinned. "It ain't so far if you're runnin'."

"He has some sense of humor, doesn't he?" Shirley commented under her breath.

While waiting for them to decide, Bud crawled onto the four-wheeler.

"We'll leave the car here and ride with you." Meggie looked at Shirley. "You okay with that?"

Shirley nodded.

"You turn that little Beetle around and hop in the back of my trailer," Bud said.

Meggie and Shirley crawled out of the Bug. They collected their berry-picking buckets, bug spray, a backpack and water cooler. They lowered the straw hats onto their heads and looked into the bed of the trailer.

"Had to transport me some manure, girls." He nodded to a pile in the trailer. "It's dried up so it won't hurt cha."

"You go first, Shirl. I'll help you in." Meggie turned away and tried not to laugh.

"It's not funny." Shirley set the berry buckets inside the trailer, stretched her leg over the metal railing and climbed in. She took the water cooler from Meggie and set it next to the buckets.

Meggie hoisted her leg over the side. She kicked the manure to the front of the trailer and leaned against the side railing.

Shirley shooed a horse fly off her foot and slapped her arm. "These darn bugs."

The four-wheeler jerked. Shirley pitched forward and swung half-way around before she caught herself. The trailer bounced along until the four-wheeler came to a stop between two boggy areas.

"Here you are, ladies." Bud shut the engine down and clambered off the machine. "Let me help you out."

Once on solid ground, the girls stood by their berry buckets and watched Bud prepare to leave. "Now," he looked from Meggie to Shirley. "How long do you wanna pick blueberries?"

They looked at each other and Shirley lifted her shoulders. "Maybe a couple hours."

"All right then." Bud waved his cap from side to side to keep the bugs at bay. "I'll be back to look for you if you don't show up in a couple hours. Stay clear of the ruts." He wiped the back of his neck with his handkerchief. "There's a good patch on both sides of the road." He pointed toward the right side. "Beyond that patch a ways it clears off and at the base of that small hill there's a rocky slope loaded with berries."

CHAPTER 24

EGGIE AND SHIRLEY WATCHED the four-wheeler bounce down the road. The trailer swayed first to one side then the other. Meggie turned to Shirley. "We better get picking." Shirley picked up her buckets and walked toward the berry patch Bud pointed out on the right side of the road. Meggie set off in the other direction.

"These berries are the size of marbles," Shirley called. "It won't take long to fill our pails."

"I hope you're right." Meggie swatted a deer fly that landed on her hand. "These bugs are driving me crazy."

"The berries are so sweet. Better than store-bought."

"Nice and ripe," Meggie shouted. "The riper the berry, the sweeter it is."

"I wonder if that goes for women."

"Huh?"

"I'd say we're ripe."

Meggie popped a firm blueberry in her mouth and savored the sweet juice. She noticed few of the berries were overripe. She cocked her ear every so often and listened for the tinkle of Shirley's bell. She filled one bucket and carried it to the side of the logging road and set it down. The second pail was almost full when Meggie realized she hadn't heard Shirley's bell in a while. She peered across the road but couldn't see her.

"Shirley!" Meggie listened but Shirley didn't reply. She held the pail up in front of her and pushed through the brush. Thorns poked at her and caught on her pants. She dashed across the road and looked around. The berry patch stood empty. "Shirley!"

"Over here." Shirley strolled into the berry patch from the direction of the hill. "I have two full buckets." She raised the buckets up for Meggie to see. "I picked over by the hill."

Relief washed over Meggie when she realized a bear hadn't carried her friend off. "Mine are full enough," she said and looked at her watch. "I know it hasn't been two hours but I'm ready to leave."

Shirley nodded. "I say we hightail it out of here before these bugs carry us off." Flies buzzed around the netting of her hat and she swatted at them. "I swear they can chew through anything."

Meggie drank from the thermos and offered it to Shirley, who tipped it up and handed it back. Meggie stuffed it into the backpack. They picked up their berry buckets and started down the road. Neither mentioned bears but occasionally Meggie scanned the woods to reassure herself there were none.

By the time they reached the car Meggie could hear the rumble of the four-wheeler in the distance. They took their straw hats off, placed covers on the berry buckets and loaded everything into the trunk of the car.

"Let's get going." Meggie slammed the trunk. "We'll meet up with Bud on the way."

Chapter 25

MEGGIE SET THE LAST PLATE in the dishwasher, secured the latch, and turned it on. The front door opened and Walter walked in the house.

"Mmm." Walter sniffed. "Something sure smells good." He tossed his cap on the recliner and marched into the kitchen.

"Blueberry pie," Meggie said.

"Atta girl." Walter threw his arms around her. "And here I thought your goal in life was to deprive me of all that was good and tasty."

"Actually, it's for Bud."

Walter's face fell. "Bud?"

Meggie reminded Walter she promised Bud a blueberry pie and related how excited he seemed about it. "I told him I would get right on it."

"I don't think that's fair." Walter pouted.

"Don't worry." Meggie laughed. "I made you a little one."

Walter turned on the oven light, bent over and peeked inside the oven. "It must be little," he said. "I can hardly see it."

Meggie felt guilty for baking him a pie, even a small pie. He had taken off a few pounds but could easily put them back on.

"I suppose I should be thankful I get a pie at all." Walter gave Meggie a quick peck on the cheek. "I think I'll take five before working on that lawn mower." He picked up the remote and sat on the recliner.

Meggie watched him flip through channels and wondered why he needed the boob tube on to sleep. She worried about his lack of exercise and grew frustrated with him when she asked him to walk with her. He had an excuse every time. She tossed the tea towel on the table. Next time she wouldn't bake him a pie at all. She glanced at the kitchen clock and picked up the phone. It rang several times before Bud picked up.

"Hi, Bud." Meggie paused. "That's the reason I'm calling." She laughed and looked at Walter. "I thought we'd stop out today." She smiled and drummed her fingers on the counter. "Right out of the oven . . . we'll see you later, then."

The timer buzzed and Meggie opened the oven door. She watched blue juice bubble out of the golden-brown pie. She set it on the rack to cool and reached in for the small pie.

Walter leaned over her shoulder. "We got any ice cream?"

Meggie thought of her stash in the back of the freezer but didn't answer him.

Walter opened the freezer door and cold air fogged around him. He crouched down and stretched his arm to the back of the freezer. "Aha." He held up a half gallon of New York Vanilla ice cream and winked at Meggie. "You hiding this, or what?"

Chapter 26

THE BUG PURRED DOWN THE HIGHWAY. Warm air blew through the open window and lifted Meggie's hair. She glanced at Walter and the blueberry pie cradled in his lap. Today belonged to him, his kind of day—blue, cloudless skies, seventy-five degrees and a slight breeze.

A cloud of dust rose in the air behind a tractor on the right side of the road, and flowers stood at attention near the farmhouse. Further on, Fish Lake sparkled like diamonds.

"Sometimes I think it would be fun to live on a hobby farm," Meggie said.

Walter arched his eyebrows. "Hobby farm?" His head moved back and forth. "You've got to be kidding."

"Just think." A grin spread across Meggie's face. "We could have a horse, maybe a cow, a few chickens." She tapped the steering wheel. "Definitely a rooster."

"A rooster?"

"No more alarm clocks." Meggie adjusted her sunglasses and glanced at Walter. "We'd wake up every morning at the crack of dawn."

"That's all I'd need." He looked at Meggie as if she had lost her mind. "A rooster crowing outside my bedroom window." He grimaced. "I'd never be able to sleep."

Meggie tilted her head to the right. "Walter snoring." She tilted her head to the left. "Rooster crowing." She grinned and turned onto the dirt road. The yellow farmhouse sprang up on her left. The same shiny, long-legged black horse nibbled grass at the base of the hill. Two black-and-white cows lay nearby.

"Better slow down. You'll knock the tail pipe off this tin can." Walter leaned out the window. "I told Bud he needs to drop a load of gravel on this driveway."

"That's spendy, isn't it?"

"He wouldn't have to do the whole driveway."

Meggie slowed to a crawl. "He probably can't afford even part of the driveway."

"I'll see what I can do." Walter shifted the pie. "I'll look into some estimates and help him out."

"He's too proud for that," Meggie said.

Walter shrugged. "We'll see."

The Bug came to a stop and Meggie killed the engine. She walked around to the passenger's side of the car and Walter handed her the pie. She waited for him to get out of the car.

Meggie raised her fist to knock when the screen door swung open. "Don't jist stand there," Bud shooed a fly out the door. "Bring that pie inside." He led the way to the kitchen, pointed to the table and sniffed the blueberry pie. "It sure smells good." He motioned Walter and Meggie to sit and took two mugs from the cupboard. He set black coffee in front of them and walked to the counter for the dessert plates and knife.

"You should keep the pie for yourself," Meggie suggested.

Bud shook his head and handed Meggie a knife. "You do the honors, young lady."

They sat around the table, visited and ate blueberry pie. Walter filled Bud in on all the latest news from Pine Lake and Bud talked about two or three mutual acquaintances. Meggie sensed Bud enjoyed company as much as he did the blueberry pie. She knew he must be lonely, living alone so long.

A worried look passed from Walter to Meggie. She, too, sensed a difference in Bud, even though she didn't know him as well as Walter did. "Are you feeling all right, Bud?" she asked. "You seem kind of down."

"Jist havin' a bit of problems but nothin' to worry about."

Walter's eyebrows raised and he tapped the side of his cup with his finger. "Anything you want to talk about?"

"Jist havin' some disagreements with the neighbor boys." Bud flipped the cover on the pie. "Nothin' worth mentionin'. I'm minding my own business for the time being."

Meggie and Walter didn't press Bud for information because it was obvious he didn't want to talk about it.

On her way out, Meggie paused in the front room near a black-and-white photograph sitting on the top shelf of the corner cabinet. "What a nice picture of your children."

Bud stared at the photograph for a long time. "Yup, sure is a nice picture of my kids." He looked at Meggie. "You and Shirley are welcome to pick more berries if you want." Bud patted his stomach and winked at her. "'Course, that means you need to bake me somethin' in return."

"It's a deal." Meggie thought a minute. "How about tomorrow? Before the berries are overripe."

"That would be jist fine." Bud pointed to an oval framed wedding picture on the wall to the right of the front door. "Celia made the best blueberry muffins." He straightened the picture and stepped back. "I can still taste 'em with butter meltin' over the sides." He turned to Meggie. "How 'bout muffins next time?"

Meggie patted Bud's arm. "Muffins it is."

CHAPTER 27

MEGGIE WALKED IN THE DOOR and set her purse on the table. She picked up the portable phone and waited through several rings. "I didn't catch you at a bad time, did I?"

"Nah," Shirley groaned. "Just a little sore and tired."

Meggie told Shirley about her visit with Bud.

"That was nice of you." Shirley spoke softly. "I bet he was thrilled to get the pie."

"He appreciated it." Meggie pounded on the deck door and chased a squirrel out of the bird feeder. "I'm picking berries tomorrow if you'd like to join me."

"Thanks, but no thanks. My back is killing me." Shirley sighed. "All that bending about did me in. On top of berry picking, I vacuumed the house when I came home."

"That doesn't sound good. How bad is your back?"

"I'm on the mend but I don't want to make it worse."

Meggie suggested she see her chiropractor and learned Bill had given her the same advice. "I'll ask Audrey and see if she wants to go." Meggie knew Audrey picked strawberries but had never been interested in blueberry picking.

"Audrey isn't home."

"That takes care of that." Meggie sat down at the kitchen table. "Do you know when she'll be back?"

"I think she planned on returning home later this evening." Shirley paused. "She and Thomas are visiting a couple they met in the square dancing club."

Meggie thanked Shirley for the information, told her to take it easy, and disconnected the call. She carried the phone to the deck and laid it on the table. She imagined herself picking blueberries alone in the middle of the woods and didn't like what she saw. She punched in Audrey's number on the portable phone and left a voice message.

Meggie leaned back and closed her eyes. A lawn mower hummed next door and kicked the smell of fresh mown grass into the air. She drifted off for a moment but was awakened by a scratching noise a short time later. She spied a chipmunk on the edge of the deck under the bird feeder. Its cheeks bulged and its eyes watched her warily. Meggie stomped her foot and it scurried down the steps and disappeared.

Chapter 28

MEGGIE WOKE TO A SILENT HOUSE. She padded to the kitchen, picked up a note from the counter and read the scribble. LEFT EARLY TO STOCK SHELVES. BE BACK WHEN I'M BACK. She tossed the note in the garbage, poured a cup of coffee and listened to a voice message from Audrey opting out of picking berries.

After a quick breakfast, Meggie packaged the blueberry muffins she had baked for Bud the previous evening. She carried the plastic container to the car, set it on the front seat and returned to the house for the rest of her gear. She climbed into the car and looked at her watch. If she hurried, she could make it to Bud's before 8:30 and into the woods before the bugs even knew she had left Pine Lake.

When Meggie called Bud the previous night, he sounded excited and promised to have coffee and donuts waiting. That didn't surprise her. Earlier in the week she stopped at Swenson's Bakery to pick up two cream-filled Long Johns for break-time at the shop, and Sandy Swenson mentioned Bud stocked up on donuts and froze them.

There were few motorists on the road so Meggie made good time. She pulled up next to Bud's truck, shut the Bug off and grabbed the plastic container of muffins. She expected Bud to greet her from the front steps but he didn't. A loud knock made her jump and her eyes darted to the woodpecker on the rotted tree.

Meggie knocked on the screen door and waited. She opened it, put her ear against the wooden door, but couldn't hear anything from inside the house. She rapped louder a second time but Bud still didn't come to the door.

The thought occurred to her he might be ill. She turned the knob, pushed the door open and stuck her head through the doorway. "Bud?" She stepped inside. "Are you home?" The atmosphere hung heavy and morning light cast streaks across the hardwood floor. She walked through the front room, into the kitchen and set the muffins on the table. Dirty dishes sat in the sink. Meggie lifted the empty coffee pot, set it down and peeked inside at the cold coffee grounds. She recalled Bud's promise to have coffee and donuts waiting for her.

Meggie checked Bud's bedroom. She found blankets strewn across the bed and a pile of dirty clothes in the corner. The smaller bedroom near the front of the house appeared untouched. Meggie searched the bathroom on her way back to the kitchen.

The door between the kitchen and screened-in porch stood open. She stepped down onto the cement floor and wrinkled her nose at the musty smell. Cobwebs hung from the ceiling and cardboard boxes lined the wall on her left. A mop and pail sat on the floor to her right and an outdated vacuum cleaner in the corner next to the mop and pail. A faded brown easy chair with boxes piled on top sat across the room near the screened side of the porch. A breeze rustled the trees and blew up dust inside the porch. A hummingbird feeder swung gently from the eaves and in the distance a dog barked.

Meggie turned around and picked up the container of blueberry muffins. She carried it to the large chest freezer against the far wall. The freezer door squealed and cold air swirled up into her face. Ice chunks hung from the freezer wall. She rearranged the frozen food and snugged the plastic container under the chocolate-covered donuts.

Meggie closed the door to the porch, hurried through the house and out the front door. She marched to Bud's truck and pulled the driver's door open. She shut it and walked past the screened-in porch to the backyard.

She opened the door on the large wooden shed and peered inside but didn't see Bud's four-wheeler. She closed it and hiked back to the Bug. She leaned against the car, put her hand on her forehead and tried to figure out why Bud wasn't home. He could have taken the four-wheeler and lost track of time, or he may have confused the day.

Meggie took a deep breath, looked at her watch and thought about her predicament. She drove to Bud's house to pick blueberries and saw no reason to change her plans. Perhaps Bud would be at the house when she finished picking and they could have coffee and donuts after all.

Meggie turned the key in the ignition and pointed the Bug toward the logging trail. She anticipated no problem finding the blueberry patch. A squirrel scampered across the road in front of the car and scurried up a birch tree. She slapped a mosquito on her face and kept a close eye on the road. She planned to drive right up to the berry patch, but if the Bug couldn't handle the road she would turn around. The car bounced up and down. She skirted the rut where it bottomed out before and slowed the car to a crawl. Several minutes later she pulled up in front of the hilly area where Shirley had picked berries a couple days earlier.

THE SUN ROSE IN THE SKY and peeked through the tops of the pine trees. One pail of plump blueberries sat on the road near the thicket and a second hung from Meggie's left hand. She batted a pesky horse fly and thought about the netted hat she forgot on her kitchen table. Deer flies attacked from behind and a mosquito whirred in her ear. She slapped at her neck, brushed the mosquito away and wiped her brow. Meggie knew she would be eaten alive if she didn't leave.

She held the pail of blueberries over her head and trudged through the brush. On the road she picked up the second pail. She packed them in the trunk, slammed it shut and slid into the front seat. Mosquitos dive bombed her from all directions. She shooed them from the car and rolled up the windows.

Meggie drove out of the woods and planned to make one last check on Bud. She parked the car in front of his house, climbed the front steps and knocked on the screen door. When there was no answer, she opened both doors and called his name. She closed them, walked to the back yard and found the shed still empty. She thought about leaving Bud a note to let him know she had been there, but decided to call him later from home.

Several yards down the driveway Meggie braked to an abrupt stop and palmed her forehead. Of course, Bud would be riding his four-wheeler on one of the logging roads. There were several in the woods so he could be on any one of them and might be in some kind of trouble. For all she knew he might have suffered a heart attack. If that were the case, Meggie knew she had to hurry or it might be too late.

She backed the car to the house but had no idea where to start looking for Bud. She walked to the shed and checked the ground for fresh tire tracks. The only four-wheeler tracks she found led to the logging road she had just driven on. She hadn't noticed anything unusual. But she hadn't been looking for anything unusual, either. It wouldn't hurt to check that road. Bud had mentioned several logging trails led off that main one. Meggie looked at her watch and realized if she planned to search the property thoroughly she needed to hurry. The thought crossed her mind that someone else took the four-wheeler, but she dismissed it.

The Bug hugged the side of the road. Meggie peered over the steering wheel and searched the woods. The car crawled by the berry patch and a short time later reached a fork in the road. Meggie brought the Bug to a stop and climbed out of the car. The road to the right hadn't seen much traffic. Tall grass grew down the center of it and brush crept over the sides. There were no visible tire marks. She inspected the road to the left and her heartbeat increased. One set of fresh tire tracks ran along the road. She surmised someone had driven this way but had not returned. She examined the tracks closer to make sure they were four-wheeler tracks and not those of a truck.

Meggie noticed something on the road several yards ahead. She hiked past a large pothole to a suspicious-looking pile. One glance told her what she already suspected. Bud had driven this way. How else would a pile of manure end up in the center of a logging trail in the middle of the woods? The manure must have bounced out of the trailer.

Meggie hiked on and wandered far from the car. She looked around and an uneasy feeling crept over her. She turned and retraced her steps to the Bug and decided to drive as far as she could.

Meggie took her time, drove around a bend and slammed on the brakes. A poplar tree lay across the road. She got out of the car to clear a path for the Bug and discovered the tree lay in sections. It appeared the four-wheeler had driven over it. She hauled the top section to the side of the road and climbed back into the car. She drove on the edge of the trail past the fallen tree and passed another no trespassing sign, but she had no intention of being deterred. Any other time Meggie wouldn't dream of trespassing, but not under the present circumstances.

Bright sun streaked through the somber woods to Meggie's left. She noticed the trees on that side of the road started to thin. She braked the car, backed up and braked again. She stuck her head out the window of the Bug and noticed smashed brush and flattened foliage. She killed the engine and pushed against the driver's door. The forest floor crunched under her feet and the smell of pine permeated the air.

An ominous feeling washed over Meggie. Something flapped overhead. She jerked her head up. A shadow crossed her side vision. She twisted around but saw nothing. She put her hand to her throat and closed her eyes. She had come this far and would not turn tail and run. If she ended up in a mess, she had no one to blame but herself. The only bright side—Shirley had stayed home.

Meggie sidestepped a large boulder and pushed aside a low-hanging birch branch. She kept her eyes pinned to the uneven ground so she wouldn't twist an ankle or worse. She ducked around a pine tree and pressed on. Sunlight streamed ahead of her and lit up the forest floor. She followed the tracks into the clearing but drew back. Several yards away stood an old weather-beaten shack, its yard overgrown with weeds and scrub.

Meggie hovered behind a pine tree and locked her eyes on a silver pickup truck parked on the far side of the shack. She couldn't see a four-wheeler but Bud might have parked out of sight. She scratched her cheek, unable to make up her mind what to do. She could walk up to the cabin and knock on the door. If she found Bud inside, she would explain the situation and all would be well. She could go home with the mystery solved.

On the other hand, if she approached the shack she might find herself in an unpleasant situation. He mentioned the neighbors were giving him problems and that someone had been harassing him. Meggie fingered a pine needle, felt it prick and let go of the branch. She stepped back and made up her mind to keep her nose out of Bud's business. He might not like her poking it in. She retraced her steps to the car and decided to call him later in the day, but her decision didn't chase away the oppressive feeling that had settled over her.

Meggie drove into Pine Lake, pulled up at Roy's Gas Station and filled the Bug. After a quick stop at the drugstore she drove to the First National Bank. She met Vera on her way inside.

"Hello, dear." Vera slipped her checkbook into her purse and snapped her purse shut. She cocked her head and took a close look at Meggie. "Are you feeling okay?"

Meggie pushed her hair back and pulled a pine needle out of it. "I feel fine." She rubbed her neck. "Why do you ask?"

"You appear a little flushed."

Meggie told Vera she had been picking blueberries at Bud Anderson's place.

"Oh, my." Vera gasped. "Do be careful in the woods. Those ticks are dreadful this year."

Meggie promised Vera she would check herself for big ticks and little ticks when she got home.

"Eldon's niece ended up with Lyme disease." Vera puckered her lips and shook her head. "Dreadful. Now it's a constant worry for her."

Meggie agreed the wood tick problem seemed to get worse every year. "I have some nice plump blueberries," she said in an attempt to change the subject. "I can bring you some the next time I come to work."

"That would be lovely." Vera patted Meggie's arm. "You know how I love blueberry muffins."

By the time Meggie arrived home it was mid-afternoon. She hadn't stopped thinking about Bud. She picked up the portable phone, punched in his number and paced the kitchen. It rang several times. She pinched the skin at her throat and looked at the clock. *Where are you, Bud?*

Meggie disconnected and punched in Lydia's phone number. "Hello, Lydia . . . fine, thanks. I've been trying to get in touch with Bud and thought you might know where he is." Meggie paused. "No, nothing important. I'll try his number later. Thanks." She laid the phone down and pushed the button on the answering machine. Walter had left a message he would be working late and planned to grab a bite to eat at the Legion. She felt relieved since she had no desire to stand in the kitchen and cook over a hot stove.

Meggie prepared a small salad for herself, carried it to the deck and nibbled at it. She pushed the lettuce around on the plate with her fork, discovered she had no appetite and strolled to the gazebo to wait for Walter to come home.

A chipmunk scurried over the walkway in front of Meggie. Overhead a blue jay floated down from the lilac tree and perched on the edge of the bird bath. She opened the sliding glass door of the gazebo, sat down on the wicker loveseat and inhaled a honeyed floral scent that drifted in through the window. Meggie watched a black squirrel scamper across the front yard and into the street. She realized how little time she spent in the gazebo and how much she missed it.

Meggie saw Walter pull in the drive close to news time and followed him into the house. He picked up the remote, sat down on the recliner and adjusted the leg rest. "They arrested some guy in Cane County for growing marijuana," he said. "The plants were worth $120,000 on the street." He flicked the station and looked up at Meggie. "They found 120 plants close to Larry's cabin."

"Bill's friend?"

Walter nodded.

Meggie waited until the commercial break to broach the subject of Bud. "Walter," she moved close to his recliner and laid her hand across the back of it.

"Hmm?"

"Bud wasn't at home today when I arrived to pick blueberries."

"And?" Walter focused on the television screen.

"And," Meggie said. "Doesn't that seem a little odd to you since he told me he would have coffee and donuts waiting for me?"

"He probably forgot." Walter played with the remote and chuckled. "Don't make a mountain out of a molehill."

Meggie's face reddened. "Now you sound like Shirley."

Walter selected another channel and lay the remote down. "You know Bud isn't as young as he used to be, and he forgets once in a while." His mouth turned up at the corners. "He probably didn't realize how important donuts were to you."

Meggie crossed her arms and glared at Walter.

"Bud's a big boy, Meg. Don't jump to any conclusions right off the bat, okay?"

"That's not all." Meggie stepped in front of the television.

Walter's voice thickened. "What's the rest of the story?"

Meggie sat on the edge of the couch. "I found this pile of manure in the middle of the woods."

Walter wiggled his eyebrows.

"I'm serious." Meggie stood, turned her back on Walter and walked onto the deck.

Walter followed Meggie and put his arm around her. "I'm sorry. What else happened?" He paused. "I want to hear the rest of the story."

When Meggie finished relating the day's events Walter threw up his hands. "That explains it. Bud forgot you were picking berries, jumped on his four-wheeler and paid a visit to his neighbors."

Meggie squinted at Walter.

"What's the matter?" He pinched her cheek. "That's not a crime, is it?"

CHAPTER 29

THE NEXT MORNING BIRDS TWEETED outside Meggie's bedroom window and sunshine filtered through the curtain. Meggie opened one eye and reached for the phone on the nightstand. She punched in Bud's number and let it ring several times before hanging up. Her stomach churned. First Ronald, now Bud. There had to be a connection.

Footsteps clomped outside the bedroom door. "Hey, you getting up?" Walter peeked in the room. "I made blueberry pancakes."

"Yeah, it's time I get out of bed." Meggie threw the sheet off and stretched her arms above her head. "You know, I think that concentrated black cherry juice helps me sleep better."

Walter cleared his throat. "Does it help you roll out of bed faster?"

Meggie stuck her tongue out.

Walter chortled and clomped away from the door.

Meggie knew he liked to poke fun but his skepticism didn't bother her. Francis told her about the concentrated black cherry juice and claimed it helped her arthritis. Francis should know, since she subscribed to several health magazines. She had forgotten to mention it made you sleep better.

In the kitchen Meggie admired the place settings and the candle burning in the center of the table, but Walter didn't fool her. He had ulterior motive stamped on his forehead. She had received inside information from Shirley the evening before, and her friend was up in arms. She warned Meggie that Bill and Walter planned to golf in the morning and worried they would spend the entire day on the course.

"Harry doesn't need me until tonight." Walter placed a blueberry pancake on Meggie's plate. "He's going to give Friday night bar bingo a try."

Meggie nodded. "What time does he need you, precisely?"

Walter sat down at the table next to Meggie. "Not until 6:30." He spread butter on his pancake and drizzled syrup across the top of it.

Meggie noted it wasn't sugar-free and realized Walter had found her stash in the back of the cupboard. She cast a sly look at him. "Since you don't work until later, do you want to hang out before you go to work?" She paused. "We could think of something fun to do. Maybe drive out to that new gift shop at Bay Resort."

Walter paused a second, then swallowed. He lifted the juice glass to his lips and emptied it. "Want more coffee?"

Meggie glanced at her full cup. "No, thank you."

Walter walked to the kitchen range and refilled his mug. "I'd really love to hang out with you, but Bill and I thought we might hit the golf course today." He set his coffee mug on the table and sat down. He leaned over his plate, forked the last piece of blueberry pancake and swished it back and forth in the syrup.

Meggie laughed. "I think that's a wonderful idea."

"You do?" Walter laid his fork on the empty plate. He tilted his head and squinted one eye. "How did you know?"

Meggie raised her eyebrows up and down.

"You don't have to reveal your source." Walter rolled his eyes. "I should have known better than to ask." He picked his plate up and walked toward the counter. "The town crier."

Meggie giggled at Shirley's nickname and watched Walter load the dishwasher. He talked about his golf strokes and shoved the final pieces of silverware in the tray. "Golfing has great therapeutic benefits."

"Uh-huh." Meggie tapped her chin. "I bet a little black cherry juice would do wonders for that golf stroke."

Walter chuckled. "You got plans for the day?"

Meggie glanced out the bay window. "I might do a little yard work."

"That's all?" Walter picked up his golf bag and didn't wait for an answer. "I'm sure you'll keep busy."

Meggie nodded. "I'm sure I will."

CHAPTER 30

A s soon as Walter walked out the door, Meggie picked up the phone. She punched in Bud's number again and let it ring seven or eight times. When he didn't answer, she lowered the phone into the cradle. The red-winged blackbird twittered from the bird clock.

Meggie dressed in a hurry and raced out the front door. She planned to stop at the Law Enforcement Center and talk to Bulldog. She drove through downtown Pine Lake, turned into the parking lot at the LEC and parked near the main door of the building.

Melanie Miller sat behind the glass-enclosed reception desk. Her head hung down and she fingered through a stack of papers.

Meggie tapped on the glass. "Good morning, Melanie."

Melanie looked up and brushed her long brown hair back from her face. "Hello, Meggie. I haven't seen you in a long time." She smiled. "What brings you here on this bright summer morning?"

"I'd like to talk to Detective Peterson if he's in."

"He was earlier. Let me check." Melanie reached for the phone and held it to her ear. She drummed her fingers on the desk. "Detective." She straightened her back. "Meggie Moore would like to speak with you if you have time." She paused. "Thank you. I'll let her know." Melanie disconnected and looked at Meggie. "He'll be out in a minute."

Meggie thanked her and waited in a chair near the long window overlooking the parking area. Heavy footsteps clomped on the other side of the lobby door. Detective Lars "Bulldog" Peterson, a large bear-like man, lumbered through it. "Morning, Meggie." He held out his hand. "You want to talk to me about something?"

Meggie stood and shook his hand. "I do, if you can spare the time."

"Let's go back to my office." Bulldog motioned her to follow.

Meggie watched Bulldog strut through the lobby door and noticed a change in the color of his hair. It appeared darker, less gray. Shirley told her he was dating a beautician who worked at Darla's Hair Fashions in Bluff. She imagined he got a good deal on a hair color.

He turned his head slightly. "Would you like a cup of coffee?"

Meggie thanked Bulldog but told him she already had her quota of caffeine for the day. She followed him down the aisle past several cubicles where uniformed deputies clicked away on their keyboards. Bulldog strode to the back of the room. He halted outside a small windowed office, stepped aside and swept his arm in front of him. "Have a seat." He followed her in and grabbed his coffee mug from the desk. "Excuse me for a second."

Meggie set her purse on the floor, folded her hands and listened to the office noise outside the door.

Bulldog returned, shut the door with his boot and sat down. He took a swallow of coffee. "Now." He picked up a pencil and tapped it against his finger. "What is it you wanted to see me about?"

"This is off the record," Meggie said.

Bulldog nodded, tossed the pencil on the desk and leaned back in his chair.

Meggie related her concerns about Bud Anderson and the events of the previous day. "The last time we spoke he mentioned having problems with his neighbors on several occasions."

"Neighbors' names?"

"The last name is Williams." Meggie explained Bud had given his grand-nephew forty acres and Ronald sold it to the Williams brothers. "My vibes tell me something's wrong."

"Mmm." Bulldog pursed his lips. "Vibrations." He leaned forward. "Let me get this straight." He picked up the computer mouse. "You arrived at Bud's house yesterday morning."

Meggie nodded.

"To pick blueberries." He paused and set the mouse by the computer. "Approximately 8:30 a.m.?"

Meggie nodded a second time. "Give or take a few minutes."

"Bud didn't greet you at the door like he usually did." Bulldog scratched his head and leaned back in his chair. "No coffee in the pot and no donuts on the table." Bulldog's lip quivered. He looked ready to laugh.

Meggie's blood pressure spiked. "That's not all," she blurted. "The truck was parked in its usual spot."

Bulldog opened his mouth to speak but Meggie cut him off. "And his four-wheeler was gone." She admitted to Bulldog she investigated and followed the four-wheeler tracks into the woods, but didn't mention she trespassed.

"There you go. Mystery solved." He lifted his hands. "Bud forgot you were picking berries and decided to talk things over with the neighbor boys."

"But—"

"Meggie, you've known Bud for as long as I have." He paused. "Maybe longer."

Meggie opened her mouth but Bulldog held his hand up to silence her. "We both know he's had an on-again, off-again relationship with the bottle for some time. That might be the reason he forgot about your donut date." Bulldog flexed his arm muscle. "Matter of fact, he's taken off before, and more than once."

"Bud doesn't drink like he did." Meggie's nostrils flared. "And anyway, he had a hard time getting over the loss of his family. That's why he started drinking in the first place."

Bulldog rubbed his ear. "How can you be so sure he doesn't drink much anymore?"

Meggie squirmed in her chair. "Bud told Walter he drinks occasionally and not as much as he used to drink." She grasped at straws and Bulldog snatched them away. "Bud doesn't lie."

"If you're that concerned, I suggest you file a missing persons report."

Meggie hesitated. "I think I should talk to his sister before I do that." She stood and picked up her purse.

Bulldog rolled his chair back.

"Meggie."

"Yes?"

"Don't get yourself into any trouble, okay?"

"You know me better than that, Detective." Meggie dug in her purse for her car keys.

"That's the problem." Bulldog's eyes lit up and a smile appeared. "I know you too well. That's why I'm telling you to stay out of trouble."

Meggie crossed her arms and recalled Bulldog from her high school days when he was a punk kid. "You mean MMOB?"

Bulldog looked confused.

"Mind my own business."

Bulldog threw his head back and hooted. "That's a good one." He escorted Meggie to the lobby and told her to call if she needed anything more. She thanked him for his time, waved goodbye to Melanie and hurried to the parking lot. She sat in the Bug and thought about her conversation with Bulldog. She glanced back at the LEC. Bulldog irritated her. He knew he irritated her and seemed to enjoy it. She picked up her phone and tried Bud's number but there was no answer. She backed out of the parking space, turned onto the street and pointed the car toward Highway 52.

Meggie didn't see Bud's truck when she pulled into the yard. She turned the Bug off, pressed her palms to her eyes and realized she had worked herself into a frenzy for nothing. Bud must have returned to the house and taken his truck somewhere. She planned to chew him out the next time she talked to him so he would know how worried she had been.

Meggie shifted the car into reverse. She started to back up but halted, killed the engine and climbed out of the car. A crow cawed and flew into a jack pine tree on the other side of the driveway. She jogged to the backyard and found the four-wheeler and trailer parked in front of the shed. The crow floated to the ground several feet away from her, cocked its black head and looked at her. Her mind whirred. She tried to recall something Bud said. She put her hands on her hips and stared at the four-wheeler. He said he locked his four-wheeler up tighter than a drum.

For her own piece of mind, Meggie searched the house one last time. The dirty dishes were still in the sink. The bedroom unchanged. Everything in the house looked the same as it had the day before. She tried to make sense of it. If he had returned to the house yesterday, wouldn't she be able to tell? And why didn't he answer the phone? Meggie concluded there must be some logical explanation. Perhaps he left at the spur of the moment and forgot to put the four-wheeler away.

Meggie drove straight home from Bud's house. She let herself in and threw her purse on the table. She picked up the portable phone, carried it to the deck and tried to get in touch with Lydia but there was no answer. She preferred to talk to Lydia so she didn't leave a message. She debated whether to call Bulldog. He would label her a busybody, but she didn't care and placed the call.

"Detective, this is Meggie Moore . . . no, that's why I'm calling. I drove out to Bud's house right after I left the LEC. He wasn't home and his truck was gone." She paused. "There's something else. His four-wheeler was parked outside the shed. Bud's a stickler for keeping that four-wheeler locked up."

Bulldog told her to think about filing a missing person's report. Meggie told him she hadn't been able to get a hold of Lydia but would try again later. She placed the phone in the cradle. Meggie wanted to believe nothing had happened to Bud, but her vibes wouldn't let her.

CHAPTER 31

AUGUST SNUCK UP ON MEGGIE. Technically it was still summer, but every year around the middle of the month the nose of fall started poking around. Meggie slipped on her walking shoes and closed the door behind her. Peppie sat on the front step with his yellow face tilted toward the sun. "Morning, my little tiger." She patted his head and hurried down the drive.

A cool breeze tousled her hair and the August sun tiptoed across her face. She stuck her nose up and sniffed the scent of fall. She looked at her watch. If she wanted to arrive at Hearts and Flowers by 8:00 she needed to beat feet.

Vera had been gearing up for the Labor Day tourist rush and her to-do list had taken on a life of its own. Meggie didn't mind the extra hours at Hearts and Flowers since she had less time to think about Bud's disappearance. She liked to keep busy but Tuesdays were usually slow.

The clanking black rattletrap interrupted her thoughts. Meggie moved over as far as she could. Leonard Johnson liked to drive on both sides of the road. The truck screeched to a stop and Leonard peered at her from inside the cab. "Mornin', Meggie."

Meggie crossed the road and stood a safe distance from the dirty vehicle. "Hi, Leonard. Are you on your way to town?"

"Told the missus I needed some adult conversation." He tipped his Minnesota Twins cap up and scratched his head. Gray hair stuck out from his scalp. Meggie had been at the Legion the night he won the Twins cap. That had been the same year Kirby Puckett made his famous catch in the outfield. Leonard saved it for special occasions, but it had seen better days. "I'm on my way to meet the boys."

"What's Francis up to this morning?"

"Busy on those blasted loons." He shook his head. "No time for me anymore."

"Come on now, Leonard. I'm sure she gives you all the attention you need." Meggie detected a blush creep up his face. "Vera claims those loons are one of her best sellers."

"Mebbe so." Leonard paused. "I s'pose you heard the news, huh?"

"You mean about someone breaking into Bud's house?"

"That's old news." Leonard leaned back and straightened his arms on the steering wheel. "Heard on the police scanner this mornin' they're searchin' near Bud's property."

"No, I hadn't heard that." Meggie waved her hand at a fly.

Leonard checked his rearview mirror. "Guess I better git before that car runs me down." The engine sputtered and the truck rattled down the road.

Meggie glanced at her watch. She had a mile to cover and needed to pick up speed if she didn't want to be late. She watched Leonard's truck shrink in the distance and thought about his news. The authorities must have information about Bud if they were searching near his property. Meggie felt confident she would be kept in the loop and could almost hear the grapevines swinging.

Vera looked up when the bell tinkled above the door. "Good morning," she said.

Meggie closed the door behind her. "You look chipper this morning."

"Francis stopped late yesterday afternoon and left this partial order of loons." Vera slid her hand into the top of the cardboard box. "She told me she included some Christmas ornaments." She pulled her hand out and held one up. "Isn't this pretty?"

"I like that." Meggie peered into the box. "You do realize there are less than 147 days until Christmas, don't you? Or something like that."

"I had no idea." Vera smiled at Meggie. "Are you counting?"

"I'm not, but Walter is." Meggie patted her pants pocket. "This time of year he holds tight to his wallet and complains Christmas shopping starts earlier every year."

Vera handed the box and loon to Meggie. "Would you mind setting them out?"

"Not at all," Meggie said. "That's what I'm here for. How about if I hang the ornaments on that small metal Christmas tree we have in the back?" she asked. "I could set the tree on the top shelf above the other loons."

"That sounds like a good idea." Vera's shoes clicked on the tile toward the rhubarb section of the shop. The ladies group from Our Lady of Lourdes Catholic Church in Pine Lake placed several rhubarb cookbooks in Hearts and Flowers on consignment. Along with the books, they left embroidered kitchen towels and aprons with rhubarb designs.

"I really do think this is one of the most interesting books I've read." Vera held up the cookbook—*Everything You Always Wanted to Know about Rhubarb*. "Most people don't know that rhubarb is actually a vegetable." She laid the book down and rearranged the embroidered towels.

"I have that book at home." Meggie set the box on the floor near the loon display. "It's a very interesting plant." She walked through the break room into the storage area and found the stepladder leaning against the back door. She carried it to the storage shelves and searched the top shelf for the metal tree.

A short time later a tiny loon swung from the top of the metal Christmas tree. "I think this looks very nice." Meggie stood back and gazed at the dainty Christmas loons.

"Let me take a closer look." Vera closed the till and clicked across the floor. "I think that's lovely. Francis does such a wonderful job." She looked at Meggie. "Of course, it goes without saying, you've displayed them very nicely, too."

The front door burst open and Shirley dashed in.

Meggie looked at her watch. Her lunch date with Shirley wasn't until much later.

"I had to stop by and see if you'd heard the news."

Meggie picked up the empty cardboard box. "You mean about the search going on near Bud's place?"

Shirley's posture fell. "Where did you hear about it? Who told you?"

"I saw Leonard on the road this morning."

"On the road?"

"I walked to work and he passed me on the way to the café."

"That figures." Shirley wrinkled her nose. "You might know that old busybody wouldn't waste time blabbing his mouth."

CHAPTER 32

T HE NEXT MORNING MEGGIE stepped out of the shower and toweled her hair. She wiped the steam from the mirror and her reflection gazed back at her. She lifted a strand of hair. Time to call Ann for another highlight. The phone rang. She wrapped the towel around herself and secured it under her arm. It rang two more times before she located it on the end table next to Walter's recliner.

"This is Lydia Erickson."

Meggie hardly recognized the soft voice. She hoped Lydia wasn't calling with bad news. "Have you heard anything about Bud?"

"The search on the property near Bud's turned up nothing." Lydia paused. "I've called to ask for help. Bud has a gun collection and several valuable antiques. His house has already been broken into once and now the public knows Bud has disappeared. It's a prime target for thieves and vandalism." Lydia took a deep breath. "Arvid and I would like to hire you to housesit for a time."

Meggie leaned against the kitchen counter. "Let me think a minute." She understood the situation and knew houses in remote locations made good targets for thieves even when someone lived in them. "Do you have any idea how long you would need me?" Meggie worried the housesitting job could drag on.

"My granddaughter, Beth, volunteered to stay at the house as soon as she ties up loose ends in St. Paul," Lydia said. She went on to say Beth had been having a difficult time since her cousin's death in Key West and had taken a leave of absence from her job. Lydia estimated the housesitting job could last up to three weeks.

Meggie knew she should talk to Walter before she gave Lydia an answer, but in the end she would do what she wanted to do. "I'll help out as long as I don't have to be at the house 24/7."

113

Lydia understood, thanked Meggie for accepting the job and ended the call.

Meggie hoped Walter would understand, too.

WALTER FOUND OUT ABOUT the housesitting job when he called Meggie from the Legion. "Let's hope Bud returns home, or at least the authorities find out where he is," Walter said. "And let's hope it's sooner rather than later."

"I'm really worried about him," Meggie said. "I don't think there's much hope in finding him alive."

Walter agreed but told Meggie it wouldn't hurt to think positive. "I better get back to work. I'll talk to you later." When he arrived home that afternoon he found Meggie's suitcase packed and loaded in the Bug.

"Lydia stopped by and dropped off the key to Bud's house." Meggie walked to the refrigerator, took out a plate of lasagna and placed it in the microwave. "I'm going to start housesitting tonight so I made lasagna for your supper."

Walter tossed his cap on the kitchen table. "I guess I don't need to tell you I'm not crazy about you taking this job." He smiled at her. "For whatever that's worth."

Meggie kissed him on the cheek. "I'll have my cell phone," she said. "I better get going so I can settle in before it gets too late."

"Are you driving into town tomorrow?"

Meggie thought a minute. "Not unless Vera calls." She paused. "I have letters to write and I'm taking my painting to work on. Why?"

"I was just wondering." Walter wrinkled his brow. "You keep the doors locked out there, you hear?"

Meggie assured him she would be fine and he had nothing to worry about. She slid her phone into her purse and caught Walter shaking his head. "What's the matter?"

"I can't figure you out." He fingered through the pile of mail on the table. "Why you want to sit out in the sticks by yourself."

"Lydia and Arvid need someone to watch the house. Besides,

it's not going to be for long," Meggie said. "When Beth arrives, she's going to take over."

Walter shoved the mail aside. "I know you want to help, but couldn't they find someone else for the job? How about Lydia?"

"Lydia said she would stay there if she were younger." Meggie gave him a hug. "I'll see you later." She didn't want to discuss housesitting with Walter. Nothing could be said that hadn't already been said a thousand times. "And don't worry about me," she called over her shoulder on her way out the door.

CHAPTER 33

THE BUG CREPT OVER THE RUTS in the driveway and rolled to a stop in front of Bud's house. Sunlight filtered through the towering pine trees and created odd designs across the hood of the Bug. Meggie killed the engine and crawled out of the car. She carried her oil painting supplies and suitcase to the front step and searched for the key to Bud's house. She fit it into the lock and pushed the door open. The old refrigerator hummed and dim sunlight danced across the shaded wood floor.

Meggie closed the door with her foot and carried her belongings to the small bedroom Lydia had prepared for her. She set her bag and painting equipment inside the bedroom door and looked around. The room consisted of a twin bed, nightstand and chest of drawers. A reading light drooped from the headboard of the bed.

A framed black-and-white photograph dangled above the nightstand. Meggie straightened it and took a closer look at the young couple. They stood outside in front of the home place. She surmised them to be Bud's parents. The pine tree to their left, now rotted and full of woodpecker holes, proudly held out its branches. She wondered how long they had been married when the picture was taken.

Meggie walked to the lone bedroom window, lifted the curtain and looked out onto the road that led to the blueberry patches. Although she couldn't see it, she knew the gate to the neighbor's property lay on the other side of the trees. Meggie had never met Bud's neighbors but she had a bad feeling about them. Bud had been pressured to sell his land and she wondered if they were the ones pressuring him. The phone rang and nudged Meggie back to the present. She let the curtain drop into place.

"Hello, Lydia." Meggie pressed the phone to her ear.

"I wanted to see if you arrived and to ask if everything was in order."

Meggie assured Lydia that it was.

"I called your house and Walter told me you decided to go out to Bud's tonight instead of in the morning."

"I hope that's all right with you." Meggie gazed out the kitchen window. "Vera asked me to work in the morning but changed her mind so I figured I may as well get moved in."

Lydia expressed her thanks, told Meggie to make herself at home and to call if she needed anything. Before she hung up, she asked Meggie to make sure everything was locked up tight.

Meggie opened the door to the screened porch and navigated the clutter on the floor. The old lock on the screen door served no purpose since anyone with a knife could cut the screen and unlock the door. She unloaded the junk from the easy chair and shoved it against the screen door. She went back into the kitchen, locked the door behind her and walked out the front door. A dog howled in the distance and a light breeze blew across her face. Meggie strode to the shed and tugged the lock on the door. It was locked up tighter than a drum.

Later that evening Meggie sat down at the kitchen table. She sipped a cup of tea and stared at two plain donuts on a plate in front of her. Lydia had been concerned Bud's donuts would be freezer-burned and told Meggie to help herself to them. She hated the thought of wasted food and loved donuts. She reached for one. "At least they aren't sugared or frosted."

Meggie finished her snack and dressed for bed. She dug in her suitcase, took out two novels and chose the cozy. She sat down on the sofa, threw her feet on the footstool and switched on the small table lamp. She became so absorbed in her book she didn't realize the sun had set and the view through the window had blackened. She stood up and stretched. *One more chapter in bed and I'll call it a day.*

CHAPTER 34

FTER WORK, MEGGIE CARRIED the carton of red raspberries to her car and set them on the passenger seat. She ached all over and rubbed her neck. The gift shop had never seen such a busy Thursday. It would be close to 5:30 by the time she arrived at Bud's house. She picked up her cell phone and called Walter to cancel her plans to stop by the house.

On her way out of town, Meggie stopped by the Soup and Sandwich Shop and pushed the door open. The scent of freshly baked bread floated through the air. A teenage girl stood behind the till and handed a brown bag to a young man. She thanked him and turned to Meggie.

"May I help you?"

Meggie studied the menu on the wall. "I'd like a cup of chicken noodle soup and a ham on rye to go, please." She observed the young lady spread mustard across the thick-sliced rye bread and set a generous piece of ham on top. She ladled soup into a large Styrofoam bowl, placed a lid on it and set the bowl in a bag with the sandwich.

The Bug purred on the way to Bud's house while Meggie's thoughts kicked about. She remembered seeing the young man at Soup and Sandwich cross the street in front of her car that morning and enter Pine Lake Café. He reminded her of the blackjack dealer at the casino. A horn honked behind the Bug and Meggie swung the car to the side of the road to let a beer truck pass.

Later that evening Meggie lay in bed and finished the last chapter of her novel. She laid it on the nightstand and reached up to turn the lamp off. A light rap sounded on the front door and her hand stopped in mid-air. Her cell phone said it was almost 11:30. Puzzled, she sat up in bed and cocked her ear. The rapping grew louder. Meggie slid out of bed, quietly crossed the front room and lifted the curtain next to the door. A dark figure stood on the step. She flipped the yard light on but nothing happened and she remembered the light bulb had burned out the previous night. "Who's there?" she called.

A soft voice replied. "It's me. Beth Erickson."

Meggie cautiously opened the wooden door and peeked out. "Beth?"

Beth sobbed. "Can I come in, please?"

Meggie flipped the front room light on. Lydia Erickson's grand-daughter stood on the other side of the screen door and wiped tears from her eyes.

"Yes, of course. Come in." Meggie swung the door wide and stepped aside.

Beth looked over her shoulder and hurried into the house.

Meggie closed and bolted the door behind Beth. "Let's go into the kitchen. Would you like something to drink?"

Beth held her hand up and followed Meggie. "No, thank you." She stood by the kitchen table. "I had to talk to someone." Tears rolled down her face and her shoulders sagged.

Meggie hugged Beth, handed her a box of tissues and gave her time to compose herself. "Sit down. I think I'll have a cup of tea." She set a kettle of water on the stove. "Whatever is the matter?"

Beth wiped her hands down her face and blew her nose. Her eyes were red and swollen. "You have to promise not to tell anyone I was here." Beth paused. "Or what I'm going to tell you."

"If that's what you want," Meggie said. "I won't tell anyone." She patted Beth's hand.

"I'm in a real mess and I don't know what to do."

"Start at the beginning," Meggie coaxed. "What kind of mess?"

Beth wrung her hands. "Maybe I will have a cup of tea, if you don't mind."

Meggie turned the burner off under the kettle and filled two cups with steaming water. She dipped a bag of Earl Grey tea in each cup and handed one to Beth. "Take your time and tell me what kind of mess you're in."

Beth took a deep breath. "Grandma told you I planned to house-sit here after I left the city, didn't she?"

Meggie nodded.

"I can't stay here because . . ." Beth pulled at the tissue in her hand.

"Because?" Meggie prompted.

"I'm afraid. I think I know who murdered Ronnie." Beth looked at Meggie. "And I think he had something to do with Uncle Bud's disappearance." She hung her head. "I should never have offered to help out."

Meggie sat back and her eyes grew round. "You think you know who murdered your cousin? Can you tell me?"

Beth lifted her head. "Jason Williams, Uncle Bud's neighbor." Shredded tissue lay strewn in front of her.

"His neighbor?" Meggie leaned forward. "The Jason who owns the land next door?"

Beth nodded. "He lives in Bluff with his brother."

"I don't understand." Meggie put her elbows on the table. "Did Jason visit Ronnie in Key West?"

"He lived there." Beth collected the pieces of tissue. "I'm not sure when he moved back to Minnesota but it was sometime after Ronnie died."

"Hold it." Meggie closed her eyes and tried to absorb what Beth was telling her. "What about Eric?"

"Eric has an apartment in Bluff. Jason moved in with him after he came back from Key West."

"I'm confused."

"See. Uncle Bud gave the land to Ronnie," Beth said. "He told him he could sell it or keep it." A tear sprouted in Beth's eye and she paused. "He wanted Ronnie to make his own business decisions. He planned to leave Ronnie another chunk of land when he died so he didn't care what Ronnie did with it."

Meggie ran a hand through her hair. "I'm following you."

"Jason and Eric were looking for hunting land so he sold it to them."

Meggie tapped her tea cup. "Why would Jason murder Ronald?"

"I don't know why, but I'm pretty sure he did." Beth pulled her purse off the back of the chair. She unzipped it, reached inside and drew out a chain. A medal dangled from it. "Stella sent me this after Ronnie died." Beth held it up for Meggie to see. "She found it in the cottage and thought it belonged to Ronnie."

Meggie fingered the sterling silver chain and looked at Beth. "It doesn't?"

Beth shook her head and dropped it into her purse. "It's Jason's. I called him and asked him about it." She teared up. "I planned to drop it off at Eric's apartment. Before I had a chance to tell him that, he told me he lost it at Ronnie's cottage a couple months before Ronnie died."

"Don't you believe him?"

"It's not true." Beth brushed a strand of hair from her eye. "I told him I saw him wearing it on Mallory Square the day before the murder and that he was mistaken." She looked at Meggie. "He got all fired up and accused me of trying to start something." Beth jutted her chin out. "He said I was trying to get back at him because he dumped me."

Meggie didn't say anything.

"We broke up a couple months before Ronnie was murdered." Beth looked down at her hands. "He used me to get closer to Ronnie."

"Jason may be a liar, but that doesn't make him a murderer."

Beth held up her hand. "It was his reaction, like he was frightened of something."

"Maybe he stopped over to see Ronald the day he was murdered," Meggie said.

"I talked to Ronnie earlier that day. He hadn't seen Jason for over a week and had no desire to."

Meggie stood and walked to the stove. She carried the tea kettle to the table and refilled their cups. She wanted to advise Beth but wasn't sure what advice to give her. "Maybe Jason just thought he lost it two months before the murder."

Beth shook her head. "That's not all."

"Did Jason threaten you?"

"Not me, but he threatened Grandma," Beth said.

"Lydia?"

"He didn't come right out and say it, but he implied it."

Meggie wondered if Beth's story could get any more convoluted.

"Before I disconnected he told me to take care of Grandma." Beth shivered. "He said old ladies have accidents."

Meggie realized Beth had no proof Jason had been involved in Ronald's death or had anything to do with Bud's disappearance, but she advised Beth to talk to the authorities. "Tell them what you've told me." She held Beth's gaze. "It won't hurt anything and it might make you feel better."

Beth refused to go to the authorities. "And that's why I can't stay here." She stood. "If Jason finds out I'm staying here I don't know what he'd do." She looked at the kitchen clock. "It's late. I should be going."

Before Beth left, Meggie told her not to worry about sitting at the house and assured her everything would work out. She promised to think of something but for now they would play it by ear. Meggie watched Beth's car bounce down the driveway. *Second night at Bud's and things are already heating up.*

CHAPTER 35

MEGGIE RANG UP THE FRIDAY purchase for the little girl. "Would you like a box?"

"Yes, please."

Meggie reached under the till and set a small gift box on the counter. The loon pin fit perfectly. She placed the box in a pale pink Hearts and Flowers bag, folded the bag and handed it to the young girl. "You have a nice day."

"My mom's waiting in the car." A smile played about the corners of her mouth. "It's for her birthday."

"I'm sure her birthday will be very happy." Meggie smiled and watched the excited child bounce out the door and into the waiting car.

The phone jingled. Meggie answered it and recognized Beth's voice. "You did?"

Vera caught Meggie's eye and pointed to the break room.

Meggie nodded and sat down on the stool behind the till. "It was the right thing to do." She paused. "You don't need to worry about that." Meggie rested her head in her hand. "Bulldog will keep it confidential. You can count on it."

The bell tinkled above the door.

"I have a customer so I have to go, but thanks for letting me know." Meggie bit her lip and wondered if she had done the right thing by advising Beth to go to the authorities. She knew it wouldn't do any good to second guess herself. At least they had been informed of Beth's suspicions. There was only one problem: Beth had no proof.

CHAPTER 36

THE ALARM ON MEGGIE'S CELL PHONE went off early Saturday morning. She reached over and felt for her phone on the night-stand. She located it, turned the alarm off and wondered why she had set it. There was no reason to get up early. Vera didn't need her at the shop and might not need her all week. She turned over and fell back asleep. An hour later her cell phone rang. She grabbed it off the nightstand and squinted at the screen. "Morning, Shirley."

"I'm not sure about that."

"About what?" Meggie's mind hadn't kicked in.

"Whether it's a good one or not."

Meggie closed her eyes for a moment.

". . . and he tried to tell me we didn't have plans and that I knew he was playing golf today." Shirley paused. "He even tried to sneak out of the house before I got out of bed. Meggie?"

Meggie yawned. "I'm here."

"Where are you, anyway?"

"Right now I'm in bed." Meggie rolled her eyes. "I'm trying to get some sleep."

"It's time to get out of bed," Shirley said. "It's almost 9:30."

Meggie opened her mouth to reply but Shirley cut her off. "I called you last night but you didn't answer." She lowered her voice. "Did you turn that phone off again?"

"I had it on vibrate until I went to bed." Meggie chuckled. "So I didn't have to take calls from pesty friends."

"Right." Shirley ignored the jibe. "Anyway, I'm heading to the casino tonight and thought you might want to tag along."

"Umm."

"Take your time. I know what's going on in that head of yours."

"You do?"

"Yes, I do. And when you get to the part where you try to con-vince yourself you shouldn't spend the money, add up all the dollars your hubbie spends golfing."

Meggie caved. "You win. I'll go but I'm not taking much money and I don't want to stay late." Meggie's good intentions to stay clear of the casino had just gone up in smoke.

"That's a good one," Shirley laughed. "How many times have I heard that?"

CHAPTER 37

LATER THAT AFTERNOON MEGGIE sat in the kitchen and waited. She drummed her fingers on the table and looked at the clock. Shirley had promised to be on time and she was a half-hour late. "Come on, Shirley," Meggie mumbled and pushed her chair back. She walked to the sink and turned the faucet on.

A horn tooted outside.

"It's about time." Meggie gulped the water and grabbed her purse. On her way through the front room she stopped by the end table and turned on the small lamp. She flipped the yard light on and pulled the door shut behind her.

The Taurus idled while Shirley stared into the rearview mirror and applied a dark pink lipstick.

"On time again, huh?" Meggie buckled her seat belt.

Shirley dabbed at her lips with a tissue. "Well, Ms. Perfect." She smacked her lips. "I had a last minute phone call, if you must know." She dropped the tube of lipstick into her purse and fluffed her hair. "So how much money did you bring?"

Meggie grinned. "I'll never tell."

"I called Audrey and invited her to go with us." Shirley shifted the car into reverse. "But you know how she feels about gambling."

Meggie knew Audrey didn't like to gamble and she didn't like to see her friends gamble either. She worried they would become addicted. The one and only time Audrey accompanied them to the casino she spent twenty dollars and felt guilty for days. "She's probably smarter than we are." Meggie opened her purse and counted her cash. "We need to call her and set a date for lunch."

"I'm always up for lunch," Shirley said and turned left on Highway 52. The Taurus picked up speed. A black Jeep Cherokee zipped past the Taurus in the passing lane. "What's that bozo doing?" The Jeep Cherokee swerved back into the right lane and cut the Taurus off. Shirley hit the brakes.

Meggie grabbed the side of the car door and jerked forward.

"He wasn't even supposed to pass. There's a yellow line." Shirley slapped the steering wheel. "Look at him. He's passing again."

Meggie's brow furrowed. "When did that car start following us?"

"I haven't a clue."

"I've seen a car like that on Bud's road more than once."

Shirley glanced at Meggie.

"Since Bud disappeared."

Shirley huffed. "If you talk to the driver tell him to hang up his keys before he kills someone." She prattled on about irresponsible drivers until the casino came into view. She slowed the car, turned off the highway and drove around the parking lot twice. "No place to park in front."

"I wonder why it's so busy?" Meggie asked.

"Senior night, I suppose." Shirley swung the car into the parking lot behind the casino. She drove down the first row and slammed on the brakes.

"Whoa!" Meggie grabbed the front of the dashboard. "Whiplash."

Shirley backed the car, braked and cranked the wheel to the right.

Meggie closed her eyes and held her breath.

The Taurus squealed and came to a stop in the parking space. "Never fear when Shirley's here." She killed the engine. "How's that for parking?"

"Aren't you a little close to the other cars?"

"Nah, we're okay the way we are." Shirley glanced sideways at the casino. "It's a little walk to the casino. I hope you're up to it."

"Are you forgetting I walk nearly every day?"

Shirley rummaged in her purse. "I know it's here somewhere." She pulled out her player's club card and shook it in the air.

"We're right next to the employee's parking lot." Meggie cracked the passenger door, carefully opened it and walked to the back of the car. "Hey, Shirley."

Shirley pointed the remote and locked the car doors. "What?"

"See that black Cherokee in the employee parking lot?"

Shirley turned around. "I see it."

"It looks like the one that almost ran you off the road."

Shirley shrugged. "There's nothing we can do about it now."

Meggie forgot about the Cherokee. "We do have a little hike to the casino, don't we?"

"Aren't you the one so concerned about exercise?" Shirley stepped up the pace. "Let's go exercise our fingers, shall we?"

Country rock blared from the loud speakers and the door man smiled. "Evening, ladies. Good luck."

"That's what I'm hoping for," Shirley quipped.

Machines dinged and lights flashed. A gray-haired woman whooped and clapped her hands at a nearby machine. A young woman in the next row appeared to be in a trance, her eyes riveted on the screen in front of her.

"What time do you want to eat?" Meggie asked.

"Let's meet about 6:30." Shirley took a quick look around and started to walk away. "If I don't show," she called over her shoulder, "I'm on a hot machine."

"The Grill?" Meggie called after her.

Shirley turned and signaled a thumbs up.

Meggie knew Shirley was on a mission and watched her hot pink top disappear into the crowd.

People drifted into the casino and by 6:30 most of the penny machines were filled. Hunger gnawed at Meggie. She strode in the direction of the Grill and hoped Shirley wouldn't make her wait for dinner. As she neared the restaurant, she spotted a hot pink shirt in a row of machines just off the Grill's entrance. Shirley glanced up when Meggie approached.

"Have any luck?" Meggie waved cigarette smoke away.

"I'm up fifty bucks." Shirley pushed the button and cashed out. "I sat down here to wait for you." She grabbed the paper ticket. "How are you doing?"

"Not bad." Meggie led the way into the Grill.

After dinner the girls agreed to play another half-hour and meet by the door. Meggie finished early and waited ten minutes for Shirley.

"A productive night for me." Shirley raised a clenched fist. "I'd love to tell Bill."

Meggie pushed through the door. "Let me guess," she said. "You're not going to tell him you won."

"That's right," Shirley said. "Why should I?"

"For starters . . ." Meggie stepped off the curb.

"He never asks how I do anymore." Shirley pulled out her car keys. "Not since that time I lost $200."

"I remember it well."

"Now he's afraid of the truth." Shirley slung her purse over her shoulder and kept pace with Meggie. "So he keeps mum."

Meggie raised her eyebrows.

"Let's say I go home tonight." Shirley stepped aside for an elderly gentleman. "I tell Bill I won."

"The honest thing to do," Meggie said.

Shirley took a deep breath. "But the next time I come out here, I lose." She looked at Meggie. "Are you following me?"

"I think so."

Shirley pressed the remote. "You don't suppose I want to tell him I lost, do you?" The lights blinked on the Taurus.

Meggie started connecting the dots. "Probably not."

"If I don't say anything," Shirley threw out her hand, "he's going to know I lost."

Meggie rolled her eyes.

"If I keep my mouth shut either way he won't know if I'm a winner or loser." Shirley pulled on the driver's door.

Meggie chuckled and shook her head. "You should have been a lawyer."

Shirley buckled her seat belt and started the Taurus. "If you think about it, I'm actually doing him a favor."

Meggie pointed out she wasn't being honest.

"What does honesty have to do with it?" Shirley asked. "Really, Meggie, you need to lighten up."

Shirley turned the head lights on, put the car in reverse and backed out. She drove to the end of the row and up the next one.

Meggie twisted around in her seat and glimpsed the black Cherokee.

Shirley made a left turn and followed the exit signs out of the parking lot.

"If the Jeep on the highway and the Jeep in the employee parking lot are one and the same . . ."

"Here we go again."

"Hear me out." Meggie rolled her window part way up. "And if that Jeep is the same one I've seen on the road to Bud's, it could belong to one of Bud's neighbors . . . Eric or Jason."

Shirley sighed. "So what?"

"It just seems odd." Meggie faced Shirley. "You know the black-jack dealer?"

Shirley nodded. "The one who looks like the panhandler in Key West?"

"I saw him tonight."

Shirley frowned. "Where is this conversation going, Detective Wannabe?"

Meggie silently mimicked Shirley's nickname for her.

"Like I said before and I'll say again . . . don't make a mountain out of a molehill." Shirley shook her head. "I don't know about you sometimes."

"Where have I heard that before?" Meggie asked.

"I'll tell you what I think." Shirley tapped the side of her head. "Maybe Bud's neighbor drives a black Jeep Cherokee. Maybe he works at the casino. Maybe he looks like the panhandler from Key West." She glanced at Meggie. "So what?"

Meggie knew Shirley had a point. She might even be right about making mountains out of molehills. "I'm just saying."

"There are millions of people in this world with two eyes, a nose and a mouth." Shirley lowered her jaw. "That might be the reason for the resemblance."

"I suppose."

Shirley threw out her hand. "I rest my case."

The Taurus pulled up in front of Bud's house.

"Come in for a cup of tea." Meggie looked at her watch. "It's not too late."

"I really should get going. It's almost dark."

Meggie opened the passenger door.

"Do you have anything to go with the tea?" Shirley asked and followed Meggie into the house.

CHAPTER 38

MEGGIE TURNED THE BURNER off under the tea kettle and reached into the cupboard.

"Don't give me that Earl Grey," Shirley ordered. "I'm getting a little tired of it."

Meggie cocked her head. "I didn't plan to."

"That's good." Shirley gazed out the kitchen window. "I probably shouldn't have caffeine this time of night, but I will."

Meggie took a package of tea off the shelf and filled the large diffuser she brought from home. She dipped it into mugs of hot water and set them on the table.

Shirley blew on her tea and sipped. "I like this."

Meggie brought the package of tea to the table and set it down. "Gunpowder green tea." She opened it. "This is what the tea looks like before it's brewed."

"Looks like pellets."

Meggie nodded. "They open up after they're brewed." She closed the package. "How about a piece of pie?"

"Ooh." Shirley's eyes glinted. "What kind?"

"Raspberry." Meggie walked to the counter and uncovered the pie. "I made it this morning. I'll save Walter a piece."

"That's torture." Shirley shook her head. "You're always on him to lose weight and the next minute you're baking something."

Meggie took two small plates from the cupboard and found a sharp knife in the drawer. "You're right. I should have saved the berries for cereal." She set a piece of pie on each plate and carried them to the table. "Then I could offer you cereal with raspberries."

Shirley slid the plate closer and picked up her fork. "I suppose Bud doesn't have any ice cream?"

Meggie took a bite of pie and shrugged her shoulders. "I didn't want to look because ice cream would just add calories."

Shirley didn't say anything.

"Do you want me to check it out?"

Shirley shook her head. "On second thought you better skip it."

Meggie lifted a large bite of pie to her mouth. At the same time her cell phone rang. She slid the fork into her mouth and pushed her chair back. She grabbed her purse off the sofa and rummaged through it. "Beth?" She strolled into the kitchen. "You're cutting out." Her brow wrinkled. "At the shack?"

Shirley glanced at Meggie, her fork suspended in mid-air. Thickened berry juice oozed down the side of the fork and dripped onto the table.

"Can you hear me now?" Meggie bit her lip. "Right away."

"What's wrong?" Shirley asked.

"Beth's back in the woods." Meggie opened the pocket of her jeans and slid the cell phone inside. "Her car is stuck."

Shirley narrowed her eyes. "The woods?"

"The neighbors."

"What in the world is she doing back there?"

Meggie took a deep breath but didn't say anything.

"And at this time of night?"

"I'm not sure." Meggie walked into the front room. "I'm going to help her get the car out."

"Need company?"

"No." Meggie reached into her purse and brought out her car keys. "Would you mind waiting until I get back to leave?"

Shirley nodded. "No problem." She picked up her plate. "Do you mind if I have another piece of pie?"

CHAPTER 39

MEGGIE SHIFTED THE CAR into reverse and backed up. At the end of the driveway she made a right-hand turn, then another right onto the neighbor's road. Meggie switched her brights on and leaned over the steering wheel. She slowed the Bug and edged past a large pothole.

The road snaked through the woods. Warm air drifted through the open window and carried dank, earthy smells. An owl hooted nearby. Meggie gripped the steering wheel and darted her eyes from side to side. She wondered what possessed Beth to drive to the shack. It was a risk since she suspected Jason of murder. The phone conversation offered little explanation. Meggie rubbed the back of her neck and focused on the road.

The Bug navigated a wide curve to the right and beyond it pine trees squeezed the trail from both sides. The Bug hit a bump and bounced around another curve. Several yards ahead Beth's Ford Focus lit up. Meggie loosened her grip on the steering wheel and parked on the road next to it. She pulled a small flashlight out of the glove compartment and switched it on. Meggie stood next to the Bug and panned the surrounding area with the light. "Beth?"

Brush crackled beyond the Ford Focus and Meggie aimed the flashlight in that direction. Beth stumbled onto the road and felt her way along the car.

Meggie hurried towards her.

"I wasn't sure it was you." Beth threw her arms around Meggie. "I'm sorry to be such a bother."

Meggie felt Beth tremble in her arms. "Never mind that." She pulled away and held Beth at arm's length. "Let's get this car out of here and then we'll talk."

"I didn't see the hole." Beth grabbed Meggie's arm. "I'll show you."

Meggie lowered the flashlight and wrinkled her brow. The chuck hole had swallowed half the front passenger tire. "Get in the car," Meggie said. She picked up the small shovel that lay beside the tire and tossed it to the side of the road. "We'll try rocking it."

"Are you sure you don't want me to push?"

"I'll see what I can do." Meggie walked to the back of the car and laid the flashlight down in the grass.

Beth climbed inside the car, started the engine and stuck her head out the window. "What now?"

"Put the car in reverse and back up as far as you can. Then drive forward."

Beth did as she was told. Meggie threw her weight against the back end of the car, pushed forward and let go. The Focus rolled back.

"Again," Meggie called.

The engine whined and the car rocked back and forth.

"Give it more gas this time," Meggie shouted and dug her feet into the ground. Rocks and dirt peppered her legs. The Focus lurched forward and cleared the hole. Meggie brushed her hands off, picked up the flashlight and peered into the driver's window at Beth. "What were you doing at the shack?"

Beth leaned her head on the steering wheel. "Snooping."

Meggie glanced towards the road and laid her hand on the door. "We better hurry and get out of here." She stepped back. "Call me to-morrow. Be careful on your way out, okay?"

"I will. Thanks."

Meggie hurried to the Bug and crawled inside. She watched the Ford Focus bobble down the road in her rearview mirror. A loud thrashing erupted in the brush to her left and made her jump. Goosebumps tingled up and down her arms. She shoved the key into the ignition and turned it. The engine knocked. She tried again but the knock grew weaker. "Great." Meggie hit the steering wheel with the palm of her hand. Walter told her to have the Bug checked over but she didn't listen to him. She took a deep breath and turned the key a third time. The engine didn't respond at all.

Meggie grabbed her phone off the passenger seat and punched in Shirley's cell phone number. CALL FAILED appeared on the screen. She pushed against the door, got out of the Bug and walked a few feet from the car. She tried the number again.

Shirley picked up on the first ring. "Where are you? What's taking so long?"

"I need your help." Meggie explained the situation to Shirley.

"Why don't we call Walter?"

"We don't have time to call Walter." Meggie was adamant. "Besides, he's working."

"What in the world was Beth doing over there, anyway?"

"I don't have time for questions." Meggie massaged her temples. "I'm sorry but I can't talk right now."

"Tell me later," Shirley said. "Should we jump start it?"

"That would work."

"I'll see if I have jumper cables."

"Don't hang up." Meggie's hand shook. "I don't want to lose the connection."

"Don't worry."

Meggie heard a door slam.

"It's pitch black except for the yard light," Shirley whispered into the phone.

Meggie heard something squeak and Shirley cussed. "The cables aren't here. I must have forgotten to put them back into the trunk when I cleaned it out."

Meggie rubbed her eyes. "Let me think."

"Should I come back and pick you up?" Shirley asked.

Meggie fell silent for a minute. "If you pick me up we'd have to leave the Bug here and I don't want to do that."

"If I had a chain we might be able to tow it but I don't have one."

Meggie tapped the phone. "Do you remember how to drive a four-wheeler?"

"I don't know, but I could try," Shirley said. "Bill let me drive his once."

"Listen carefully." Meggie directed Shirley to the drawer below the silverware. There she would find a ring of keys. The key marked with black tape would open the shed. White tape marked the four wheeler key.

"I'm on it."

Meggie paced, held the phone to her ear and waited for Shirley to come back on the line.

"I'm ready." Shirley panted. "I'm sitting on the machine right now and turning it on."

Meggie heard the machine rumble before the line went dead. She crawled into the Bug, took a deep breath and tried to stay calm. Minutes ticked by. She checked the time on her phone. Ten minutes passed since she had called Shirley.

A narrow set of headlights lit up the driver's sideview mirror. Meggie laid the phone on the passenger seat and stepped into the night. The lights grew brighter and bobbed up and down. They disappeared, popped up, slanted to the right, then to the left. They bounced up and dipped. Meggie held her breath and prayed her friend knew which way to lean.

Shirley shouted but Meggie couldn't understand what she said and the headlights disappeared. Seconds later the machine roared down the driveway. It rattled past Meggie and came to an abrupt stop several feet in front of the Bug.

"I'll back up," Shirley shouted.

Meggie heard the gear grate and the four-wheeler reversed. It shot past Meggie and jerked to a stop several feet in back of the Bug. Meggie exhaled, aimed the flashlight on Shirley and ran towards the four-wheeler.

Shirley stood and tried to swing her right leg backward over the seat of the machine. "I need some help here." She tugged at her leg. "These doggone pants are too tight."

Meggie reached up and dislodged Shirley's leg. "Sit down and swing your leg over in front of you."

Shirley sat back, picked up her leg and lifted it to the other side. "It must have been that last piece of pie. The pants tightened up on me." She jumped down and looked skyward. "Whew. Count your blessings. I made it in one piece and so did the four-wheeler."

Meggie squatted and aimed her flashlight at the front of the machine. "The four-wheeler has a winch." She ran a hand through her hair.

"What's that?" Shirley peered over Meggie's shoulder.

Meggie lifted a large hook. "Here's the cable." She stood and strode toward her car. "Let's take a look at the Bug." Meggie got down on all fours and looked under the back bumper.

"Are we pulling it back to Bud's?"

Meggie looked up at Shirley. "We're going to try." She pointed underneath the Bug. "I think you should be able to secure the cable right there."

Shirley squatted down to see what Meggie pointed at.

"Wait here," Meggie said. "I'll pull up to the back of the Bug and release the cable."

"What do you want me to do?"

"Grab the cable." Meggie climbed on the four wheeler. "Hook it on the Bug where I showed you." She turned the key and hit the headlight switch.

Shirley shielded her eyes from the glare of the headlights. "What are you in such a panic for?"

The machine moved forward and closed the distance between the two vehicles. "We don't want to get caught trespassing."

"Yeah, right." Shirley threw up her hands. "And cows fly. There's more to it than that."

Meggie pushed a button that set off a loud grinding noise.

Shirley grabbed the cable and hooked it under the Bug.

"Make sure it's secure. Hurry, please."

Shirley tugged at the cable. "It should hold." She put her hands on the bumper of the Bug and pushed herself to a standing position. She scurried to the driver's door and grabbed the handle. "Aren't you ever going to fix this?"

"Push in a bit and then pull." Meggie waited for Shirley to get settled in the Bug. She put the four-wheeler in reverse and pushed the hand throttle. The machine reeled backward. The Bug's back end rose, then fell.

The driver's door opened and Shirley stumbled out. "What happened?" She watched the cable snake across the ground towards the front of the four-wheeler. "You got any other good . . ."

"What's the matter?" Meggie followed Shirley's gaze.

"I think I saw lights shine through the trees."

"What?" Meggie's stomach pitched. "I don't see anything. It must have been your imagin—" She inhaled sharply. "Get in the car," she shouted. "I'll hide the four-wheeler."

"What about the Bug?" Shirley yelled.

"We'll push it out of sight."

Meggie drove around the Bug with the four-wheeler. She aimed for a small clearing between two spruce trees, bent low and plowed through. Needles pricked and prodded her skin. The four-wheeler hit a rut and stalled. Meggie bounced in the air, fell forward and back onto the seat. She hit the start button and pushed the throttle. The tires spun. The machine lurched forward and squealed to a stop a few feet away. She shut the machine off and jumped to the ground. Her heart hammered in her ears. She reached inside her bra, took her flashlight out and switched it on.

Meggie waded through the underbrush and felt its tentacles wrap around her legs. She tottered, fell backwards and lay buoyed on the brush. She twisted out of its grasp, raised her arms and charged through the pines. She reached the clearing and staggered toward the Bug.

Shirley sat with the door open and started to stand. "Are you all right?"

"Stay in the Bug. I'm fine." Meggie looked down at the blood oozing from her arms. "Make sure the car's in neutral."

"Roger."

Meggie stood in front of the car. "Turn the wheel to the left. We have to back it up."

Shirley cranked the wheel to the left.

Meggie pushed, shoulder to metal. The Bug moved backwards. "Okay," she shouted. "Straighten the wheel and I'll push from behind." She bent down, dug her shoes in the dirt and pushed. The Bug inched forward. She straightened up and wiped her palms on her jeans.

Shirley peeked out the window. "Want me to get out and help push?"

"You'll have to. It's too much for me."

Shirley scrambled out of the Bug.

"Steer with your right hand." Meggie glanced down the drive. Lights flickered through the trees. "The lights are getting closer."

Shirley kept her right hand on the wheel and her left on the door of the Bug. "Let's move it," she shouted.

Meggie took a deep breath, bent low and dug in. Her feet slid in the grass. She pushed harder, felt her face tingle. The Bug picked up momentum and rolled to the edge of the spruce trees. "Push it through," Meggie shouted. She turned her head and watched the lights spread over the trees. "Push harder. Hurry."

The spruce branches scraped the body of the Bug.

"Ouch." Shirley moaned. "These needles hurt."

"Duck down, we're almost there." The Bug cleared the trees. "Stop now. Don't hit the rut." Meggie looked over her shoulder, heard a rumble. "Turn the wheel to the left. We'll move it a couple more feet." Shirley groaned, pushed harder and the Bug rolled to a stop.

Meggie bent down, peered through the branches behind her. Bright light exploded onto the road where the Focus had been parked. She crept to Shirley and touched her shoulder. "We can't make a sound," she whispered.

Shirley nodded and didn't move.

Brakes squealed, a door slammed.

Meggie leaned forward and cupped her ear.

"What the . . ." The voice was barely audible.

Meggie squatted and peered through the branches of the spruce tree. Headlights beamed from a truck onto a black figure. The figure held something and moved out of the light. Meggie heard a clunk, rattle. Her hands trembled. *Beth's shovel.*

A door slammed and the vehicle rumbled on.

Shirley backed into the driver's seat and plunked down.

Meggie hurried to the passenger side and crawled in.

"What are we going to do now?" Shirley sounded frightened.

"Wait until the truck leaves." Meggie held her breath and listened. Far off a door slammed. She twisted around in the seat and peered through the Bug's back window. The night looked black as the ace of spades. "The truck must have gone deeper into the woods." A low rumble sounded in the distance and grew louder.

"Sounds like it's coming back," Shirley said.

Meggie glimpsed lights flicker across the trees. The rumbling grew louder and the truck shot down the drive.

"I wonder what's going on?" Shirley stammered. "Do you think we should make a break for it?" She put her hand on the driver's door.

"No." Meggie checked the time on her phone. "We'll sit here and give the truck time to get out of the woods."

Brush crackled close to the car. "What's that?" Shirley sat up in her seat.

"Probably squirrels." Meggie sat back and waited.

After a few minutes Meggie picked up her cell phone and checked the time again. They had been in the woods almost twenty minutes. She scanned the area and looked at Shirley. "We'll have to leave the Bug here." She nodded at the four-wheeler. "We'll ride that to Bud's house." Meggie threw up her hands. "I'll have to call Walter to pull the Bug out of here. He's home from work now."

Meggie pushed her way through the thistles and scrub. She climbed on the four wheeler and held out her hand.

Shirley grabbed Meggie's hand and mounted the machine. "Let's get the heck out of here," she said. "I want to go home."

Chapter 40

Meggie waited until Shirley left to call Walter. "The Bug is where?" Walter barked into the phone. "You want me to bring the truck out tonight?"

Meggie looked at the clock. "I'm sorry, I know it's late."

"Late?" Walter growled. "It's almost midnight."

Meggie bit her lip and gave Walter an account of what had taken place earlier in the evening. "I don't want to leave it there. I could get in trouble." She pressed the phone to her ear. "What did you say?"

"Never mind."

Meggie heard the bed squeak.

"I'll be there in about twenty minutes," Walter said.

"Thanks. I love you."

"Wait a minute," Walter said. "One question."

"And that would be?"

"What business did Beth have in the middle of the woods at this time of night?"

"I'm sorry but—"

"None of my business, right?"

Meggie straightened her back and didn't reply.

"Hope you're not up to your old tricks," Walter said.

"If you must know, I'm not sure what she was doing in the woods."

"Translated," Walter said. "You know something you're not telling me." He told Meggie he would see her in a bit and disconnected.

Meggie pushed her chair back. "Old tricks." She left her phone on the table and walked into the front room. "He makes me sound like I'm some kind of dog." She sat down on the sofa, threw her feet onto the footstool and laid her head back.

A short time later she woke to a loud rap on the front door. She sat up and rubbed her eyes. "Walter?"

"Yeah, it's me," he said in a loud voice.

Meggie opened the door.

"Who else would be rapping at your door in the middle of the night?" He pecked Meggie on the cheek. "Were you expecting some tall, dark and handsome hero?"

"Better mood?" Meggie smiled. "I'll settle for not so tall, starting to bald and attractive."

"Ready?"

She patted her pocket for the house key. "Let's do it."

Twenty five minutes later they returned. "I hope you're not doing anything you'll be sorry for," Walter warned.

Meggie didn't say anything. It had been a long day and she didn't want to be interrogated.

"Where do you want me to sleep?" Walter peeked into the small bedroom.

Meggie followed close behind. "Want to snuggle?"

"Thanks, but no thanks." Walter backed out. "My snoring would blow you out of that bed."

Meggie offered Walter the large bedroom but he said he wouldn't feel right sleeping in Bud's bed. He nodded at the sofa. "I'll sleep right there."

Meggie found a sheet in the bathroom closet and a blanket and pillow in Bud's room. She made up the sofa and kissed Walter goodnight.

The clouds disappeared and moonlight filtered through the bedroom window. Meggie lifted the curtain and looked out on the strange glow that spread over the trees. Shivers ran down her spine and she dropped the curtain. *What business did Beth have at the shack, and will she tell me?*

WALTER TOWED THE BUG to Benny's Auto Repair the next morning. Benny promised him one of the guys would be on it first thing Monday morning. After they attended Mass, Walter surprised Meggie with breakfast at Pine Lake Café. Belle had just taken their order when Meggie's cell phone rang.

"I'm so sorry I involved you in my mess," Beth said. "It was foolish of me to go to the shack."

"What were you looking for?" Meggie asked.

"I wanted to find something that tied Jason to Ronnie's murder or Uncle Bud's disappearance. It was a long shot."

"And did you find anything?" Meggie asked.

Beth cut the call short and didn't give her an answer. Meggie suspected Beth was keeping information from her but knew there was little she could do about that for the time being.

CHAPTER 41

EGGIE GAVE WALTER A WAKE-UP call early Monday morning since he promised to give her a ride to work. Coffee steamed from her cup. She carried it to the kitchen window and lifted the curtain. The rain left two large puddles beyond the lilac tree. Meggie set her coffee mug on the table. She pushed up on the wooden window frame, inhaled the fresh air and made a mental note to open the other windows after work.

Meggie sat down at the table and nibbled on a slice of toast. She checked the clock and hoped Walter wouldn't be late. Vera expected her at Hearts and Flowers no later than 10:00. She sipped her coffee and thought about Beth's phone call and wondered what her young friend was hiding.

A horn honked, startling Meggie back to the present. She set her dishes in the sink, slid her cell phone into her purse and locked the door behind her. *What would Walter do without a horn to honk?*

VERA HANDED MEGGIE a list of duties. "Would you mind if I handle the till today?"

Meggie thought Vera looked peaked. "Are you feeling all right?"

"A little tired is all."

Meggie took the list, waved it and turned to go. "I'll get busy and if you want to go home, just say the word."

Vera nodded. "I'm sure that won't be necessary."

Meggie worked with inventory and cleaned the break room. She crossed off the first two items on the to-do list and set the list on the break table. She filled the electric pot with water, plugged it in and carried a box of handmade note holders to the front of the shop.

145

Sandy Swenson stood at the till ready to check out and looked flustered. "Did you take the day off, Sandy?"

"Hardly." Sandy narrowed her eyes. "Randy wants to leave the bakery early today. He says it's an emergency."

Meggie's eyebrows shot up. "Emergency?"

"Emergency on Spirit Lake." Sandy crossed her arms. "Leonard told him the sunnies are biting."

"I hear ya," Meggie grinned. "Food for the table, huh?"

"That husband of mine better bring home a mess of fish." Sandy forced a laugh and picked up her package. "That's all I can say." She waved goodbye and scooted out the door.

"How about a break?" Meggie asked.

Vera nodded. "I think so."

Earl Grey steamed from their mugs and raspberry muffins heated in the microwave. The door to the shop flew open and the bell chimed.

"Meggie!" Shirley shouted.

Meggie set her cup down and scurried to the front of the shop. Shirley stood near the door, her face flushed. "Shirley." Meggie took her arm. "What is it?"

"They were searching . . ." she stuttered.

"You better come in and sit down." Meggie helped her to the stool behind the till. "You don't look so good."

Shirley's hand shook. She plucked a tissue from the box near the phone.

Vera's shoes clicked on the tile. "Whatever is wrong?" She edged near Meggie and stared at Shirley.

"Terrible news." Shirley sniffed. "Bill called me on my cell phone right after Leonard called him."

Meggie's pulse quickened. "Bud?"

"They found a body." Shirley wiped her forehead with a tissue. "At Bottomless Lake."

"Oh, dear." Vera swayed against Meggie.

"I'll grab a chair," Shirley said and jumped off the stool. She ran into the break room and returned with a chair and wet tea towel.

Meggie held onto Vera to keep her from falling and helped her into the chair. Shirley placed the wet towel across her forehead.

Vera sat still and closed her eyes. "Don't fuss girls, I'm fine." She straightened her skirt and peeked at Shirley from underneath the wet towel. "Do tell us what you know."

"I was in my car when Bill called me," Shirley said.

"I suppose Leonard heard about the search on his police scanner." Meggie removed the towel from Vera's forehead and wiped the sides of her face with a tissue. "He didn't actually see anything, did he?"

"Yes, he did." Shirley's head bobbed up and down. "He watched them pull the truck out of the lake and he saw the body bag."

"He saw them?" Meggie knew the area would be off limits.

"With his own two eyes." Shirley sat down on the stool and set her elbows on the counter. "He parked across the lake and used his binoculars."

Meggie's stomach turned. "Bottomless Lake must not be bottomless after all."

Shirley cleared her throat. "Whoever dumped the truck there didn't know that."

"It might have been an accident." Meggie walked to the phone to call Walter.

"I don't think so." Shirley picked up her purse. "It wasn't near the main road."

"He could have driven off the road." Meggie looked at her friend. "We don't know for sure if it's Bud or not."

Vera fidgeted. "We must be prepared for the worst." She took hold of the towel and stood up. "But now we must get back to work."

CHAPTER 42

WALTER PICKED UP ON THE FIRST RING. "I've heard. Leonard called with the news." He spoke in a low voice. "The body will have to be identified." He paused. "They'll probably do an autopsy."

Meggie's chest ached. She told Walter she would talk to him later and set the phone down. She looked at Vera and excused herself. In the break room she let the tears flow.

Vera followed Meggie to the break room and threw her arms around her. "There, there." She patted Meggie's back. "Let's just wait and see what the authorities find out."

"I'm sorry." Meggie wiped her eyes and blew her nose. "I feel so bad. It's all so horrible."

Vera suggested Meggie take the rest of the day off and go home to rest.

Meggie shook her head. "I'm not leaving you." She stood and parted the curtain to the gift area. "I'm in no hurry to return to Bud's house. I'll stay until closing."

The sun hung low in the sky by the time Meggie turned onto Bud's driveway. She slowed the Bug and took her time. A deer stepped onto the road a few feet in front of her. She braked the car. The deer fixed its large, soulful eyes on her and twitched its tail. It crossed the road, bounced over the ditch and into the woods.

Meggie parked the car, gazed at Bud's house and thought about the horrible turn of events. Bud missing. A truck pulled out of Bottomless Lake. A body. She shook the cobwebs from her mind, took a deep breath and stepped out of the Bug. Warm air hung thick around her. A rabbit scampered into the woods. Meggie looked for the woodpecker but didn't see it. She thought about Bud and his love for the forest and animals.

Meggie wiped her hand across her eyes and mounted the front steps. She fished in her purse and pulled out her keys. She lifted the house key to the lock and drew back. The door hung open. Her heart raced. She remembered locking it before she left that morning. She stood a moment on the step and listened. Then pushed the door with her finger. It creaked open.

Meggie stood in the doorway and scanned the front room. Nothing seemed amiss. The refrigerator hummed and late afternoon sun streaked across the hardwood floor. She stepped inside but left the front door ajar. She searched the house but found nothing to indicate anyone had intruded. The shrill ring of the telephone startled her. She hurried to the kitchen to answer it.

"Hi, Shirley. I just walked through the door." Meggie took a glass out of the cupboard and filled it with water. "You don't have to. I told Walter not to worry about it." She took a drink. "Sure, if you want to. I could use some company." A small bird flew by the kitchen window. "All right. I'll see you in a bit."

Meggie changed into lounge wear and grabbed her book off the nightstand. In the kitchen she brewed a cup of tea and carried it to the table. She opened the novel but found it hard to concentrate and set it aside. Someone had been in the house. She rubbed her temples and a thought struck her. Lydia had a key and so did Beth. She sagged against the back of the chair and berated herself for worrying. It must have been one of them. She picked up the phone and punched in Lydia's number. The phone rang several times before Lydia picked up.

"No. I've been in bed most of the day." Lydia sounded tired. "Is something wrong?"

Meggie told Lydia she found the door unlocked when she arrived at the house after work. "I must have forgotten to lock it," she said and hoped Lydia wouldn't worry. Afterwards Meggie punched in Beth's number, but there was no answer.

Tires screeched outside, a car door slammed and the front door opened. "Anyone home?"

CHAPTER 43

MEGGIE EJECTED THE DVD and handed it to Shirley. "That was good." She smiled. "Better than I expected."

Shirley held out her hand for the DVD. "Nothing like a chick flick to get you out of the doldrums."

"You might be right." Meggie scratched her head. "Are you hungry?"

"Depends on what you have to eat." Shirley followed Meggie into the kitchen and sat down at the table. "Got any donuts left?" She picked up the salt shaker and set it back down.

Meggie's eyes narrowed. "You really don't think I gobbled up Bud's supply of donuts, do you?" She walked to the cupboard and opened it up.

Shirley grinned. "I never know about you."

"Coffee or tea?"

Shirley put her finger to her lip. "Got milk?"

Meggie threw her shoulders back. "Of course I have milk." She stood on tiptoe and took two tall glasses from the cupboard shelf. She noticed a crack down the side of the second one, set it on the counter and reached for another.

"I'll get the donuts." Shirley shoved her chair away from the table and walked into the screened-in porch.

Meggie set the glasses and carton of milk on the table.

"Good thing Bud has a microwave," Shirley called, "or these donuts would be harder than a turd."

Meggie heard the freezer door squeal and seconds later Shirley shouted. "Meggie! Come here!"

Meggie stepped into the porch. A hand gun dangled from Shirley's index finger. "What on . . . where did you find that?"

"Under the chocolate-covered donuts." Shirley looked frozen, her eyes round. "I was looking for the chocolate sprinkled."

"Don't put any more fingerprints on it." Meggie's mind whirred. The chocolate-covered donuts. She moved them the day she made room in the freezer for the blueberry muffins. There had been no gun then. "That doesn't belong to Bud." She peered into the freezer. "Bring it into the house and we'll put it in a bag."

"Whose is it?" Shirley trailed Meggie into the kitchen. "How did it get in the freezer?"

"That's what I'd like to know." Meggie bent down and opened the cupboard door. She took a box of freezer bags out and handed one to Shirley. "Wipe your prints off and drop the gun in this bag."

"I only touched one spot." Shirley reached for a tissue from the box on the counter and wiped her prints off. She dropped the gun into the bag, zipped it and set it on the table.

Meggie picked up her cell phone.

"Who are you calling?" Shirley sidled up to Meggie.

"Beth."

"Why are you calling her?"

Meggie held up her hand. "Beth?" She closed her eyes for a second. "It's Meggie . . . I'm sorry . . . I know." Meggie brushed a strand of hair from her eye. "I'm at Bud's. Did you happen to stop by here today?"

Meggie paced the front room and Shirley shadowed her. "You did what?" Meggie stopped pacing and put her hand on her forehead. "What on earth were you thinking?" She paused. "When did you plan to tell me?" She looked at Shirley, sat down on the couch and put her elbows on her knees. "Shirley's here but she won't say anything. I'll go with you." She stood. "Right away. Tonight."

CHAPTER 44

I DON'T THINK I WANT to hear it." Shirley threw her hands on her hips. "But tell me anyway."

"Beth said to fill you in, but you can't breathe a word of what I'm about to tell you."

Shirley signed her heart. "Cross my heart and hope to die. Stick a needle in my eye."

Meggie scowled. "Be serious. Promise me."

"Oh, for heaven's sake," Shirley snarled. "You'd think I was some kind of big mouth."

Meggie folded her arms across her chest.

"I promise." Shirley pursed her lips. "Is that better?"

Meggie nodded and related Beth's suspicions. ". . . and that's why she stole the gun."

"Stole the gun?" Shirley followed Meggie into the bedroom. "The night she got stuck in the woods?"

"I'm afraid so." Meggie walked to the chest of drawers. "She took it before they found the body at Bottomless Lake."

"What was she thinking?" Shirley's eyes blinked.

"It wasn't a smart thing to do." Meggie opened a dresser drawer and fingered through it. "Now the authorities have a body. If he's guilty of anything . . ."

"He's going to get rid of the gun." Shirley sniffed. "Even I know better than to tamper with evidence." She flicked a piece of lint off her shirt. "Young people don't use common sense."

Meggie held up a flashlight and switched it on and off. "Beth wasn't thinking. She thought it could be used as evidence in Ronald's murder or maybe Bud's disappearance."

"And now she's returning it?" Shirley shook her head.

"Beth realized her mistake and drove over this morning to return it. When she turned on Bud's driveway, she saw Jason's truck come out of the woods and got scared. She knew if he discovered the missing gun, he might try to search her car. She didn't want to get caught with it."

"So she hid it in the freezer and forgot to lock the front door."

Meggie nodded, slid the drawer shut and cocked her ear. "I think that's her now." She turned the bedroom light off. "We're returning it tonight."

"*We're?*" Shirley hurried after Meggie.

A loud rap shook the front door.

"Just a minute." Meggie drew the bolt and swung the door open.

Beth stood on the step, her hair disheveled. "We have to hurry." She wrung her hands. "Eric's at the casino now."

"Casino?" Meggie thought about the blackjack dealer.

"He's dealing tonight." Beth fidgeted. "Allie told me."

Meggie's stomach tightened. "Allie?"

"Eric's girlfriend. She called me from his apartment." Beth shuffled her feet. "We really have to go."

"What about Jason?" Meggie hesitated.

"Jason's going to some meeting in Cane County."

Meggie arched her eyebrows.

"Okay. I had Allie fish for information. She doesn't like Jason, either."

"We'll take the Bug." Meggie walked toward the kitchen. "I'll get the gun. We'll leave a light on in the house."

Shirley stood in the middle of the room. "What about me?"

Meggie picked the gun up from the kitchen table and carried it into the front room. "You can wait here if you want."

Beth shifted her feet.

Shirley glanced outside. "I'm not sure I want to stay here by myself." Her lips trembled.

"Make up your mind," Meggie said.

"I'll go."

Meggie handed the gun to Beth. "Let's do it." She followed Beth and Shirley outside and locked the front door behind her.

"Give me a minute." Shirley hustled to the Taurus.

Meggie climbed in behind the wheel of the Bug and started the engine.

Beth opened the passenger door but waited outside the car. She leaned down and peeked in at Meggie. "What's she doing?"

Meggie shrugged.

The Taurus door slammed and Shirley made a beeline for the Bug. She held up a bat and shook it. "Just in case, and it's aluminum."

CHAPTER 45

THE TALL PINES GLOWED in the bright headlights and shadows hovered across the road.

"Why are we going this way?" Shirley asked from the back seat.

Beth turned around. "We don't want to take any chances of being seen, just in case."

"Chances?" Shirley's voice broke. "Of being seen just in case of what?"

Meggie leaned over the wheel and studied the road ahead. "It's a pretty safe bet Jason or Eric won't visit the shack tonight, but we have to be careful." She glanced in the sideview mirror. "We'll leave the Bug on the trail where it won't be visible."

The Bug rolled past the berry patch. "The fork's up ahead," Meggie said. She dodged a sink hole and stepped on the brake. Two eyes glowed near the ground on the side of the logging road. A skunk waddled across in front of the Bug and disappeared into the brush. Meggie drove on and decreased speed when she approached a bend.

"There's the fork." Shirley sat forward in her seat. "And another no trespassing sign."

Meggie tapped the brake and cranked the wheel to the left. "It won't be long now." The Bug bounced and hit a pothole. It traveled a distance before Meggie stuck her head out the window and slammed on the brakes.

Beth jerked forward and grabbed the dashboard.

Meggie slid the car into reverse and backed up. A large boulder sat on the left side of the road. "Here's where we get out." Meggie looked from Beth to Shirley. "Ready?"

Beth clutched the plastic bag in her left hand and the door handle in the other. Her flashlight stuck out of her shirt pocket. "Ready."

Meggie turned and faced the back seat. "Shirley?"

"Maybe I'll wait here." Shirley peered into the dark woods and gripped the bat. "I might slow you down." She looked at Meggie and Beth. "You don't mind, do you?"

Meggie shook her head. "No. You have your phone, right?"

Shirley held up her cell phone. "I brought a flashlight, too."

"It'll take us a few minutes but it's a pretty straight shot to the shack. We shouldn't be long," Meggie said. She pushed against the driver's door and turned to Beth. "Follow me." She stepped out of the Bug and switched the flashlight on.

Beth walked around the front of the car. "It's black out here."

Meggie sidestepped the boulder and aimed her light on the trail. She pushed aside the birch branches and hunched low. The scrub crunched and snapped. She guarded her face against the sharp pine needles and inhaled their fragrance. They pricked her hands and arms. Meggie patted her pocket and turned to Beth. "I forgot my cell phone."

"I have mine," Beth said.

A howl rose in the air.

Beth flashed her light from side to side and whispered. "What's that?"

Meggie stood still and listened. "Sounds like a coyote."

Beth gasped and bumped into Meggie. "Coyote?"

"Don't worry." Meggie plodded on. "They won't hurt you."

"How do you know?" Beth grabbed Meggie's shirt.

"Walter told me."

"I hope he knows what he's talking about."

Meggie gulped. "Me, too."

The brush cleared. Meggie aimed her flashlight on the ground in front of her. She walked several more yards, raised the light and swept it from side to side. "There it is." The hunting shack stood several yards to her right. "Let's hurry."

Beth pushed ahead of Meggie, navigated a small patch of brush and darted through the clearing toward the shack. The light from her flashlight bounced up and down.

Beth stood on the step and struggled with the door lock. "Darn." Her flashlight dimmed and went out. "No battery." She dropped it on the step next to the gun.

Meggie focused her flashlight on the door lock.

Beth's hand shook. She slipped the thin nail into a tiny hole in the center of the lock and pushed. The lock clicked. She turned the knob and pushed the door. It creaked open. She dropped the nail into her pocket, bent down and retrieved the gun.

"Take this." Meggie held out her flashlight.

Beth took the flashlight and entered the shack. She flashed the light left to right.

Meggie glimpsed a wood heater in the corner of the room and an old couch against the far wall. The couch had no cushions and its stuffing hung out.

Beth moved and the floor boards creaked. "I found the gun in Uncle Bud's hiding spot." She walked past an old wood cook stove on the left and twisted her head toward Meggie. "He hid his booze there when he was a kid."

Meggie kicked an empty can out of her way and followed Beth into a cramped room. She brushed a spider's web from her face and rubbed her hand down her jeans.

Beth led the way across the room and stopped. She kicked a worn braided rug to the side and knelt on the floor under the window. She handed Meggie the flashlight. "Can you shine it down here?"

Meggie stepped over the corner of a bare mattress lying in front of her and pointed the light on the rough wood floor near Beth.

Beth took a small knife from a pocket near the cuff of her pants and opened it. She shoved the blade under a plank of floor board, jimmied it loose and set it aside. She did the same with the board next to it.

Meggie lowered the light.

Beth's hand disappeared into the hole in the floor. She moved it back and forth. "The box is still here." She slid the gun out of the bag and into the box under the floor. "Not a good place to store a gun. He must have been desperate."

"He was probably in a hurry." Meggie inhaled sharply. Lights flickered on the wall. "I think someone's coming."

"We have to hide." Beth shoved the boards in place and jumped up. "It's too late to run out the door."

Meggie's stomach clenched. She passed the flashlight to Beth and stepped in front of the window. She leaned forward and shoved against the window frame. "It's stuck. Help me."

Meggie and Beth threw their weight against the top of the window frame and strained against it. The frame moved and the window slid open.

Meggie cupped her hand. "Give me your foot." She heard a rumble in the distance.

Beth hesitated.

"You're shorter." Meggie glanced over her shoulder and back at Beth. "Now."

The tree tops grew brighter, the rumble louder. Meggie's heart raced.

Beth tossed the flashlight through the window and grabbed the sill. She placed her right foot in Meggie's cupped hand.

Meggie braced her legs, straightened and boosted Beth up.

Beth wrapped her left leg around the opening and sat sideways on the sill. She leaned to the left, pulled her other leg through the window and dropped to the ground.

Meggie swung her leg up and caught the edge of the sill with her foot.

The headlights disappeared and a door slammed outside.

Meggie grasped the sill and hoisted herself up to the opening.

The shack door groaned and floor boards creaked. A light bounced around the shack. Footsteps pounded toward the bedroom.

Beth grabbed Meggie around the waist and pulled her to the ground. Rocks and nettles poked Meggie and her heart hammered. She reached for Beth's hand and felt it tremble.

Beth whispered in Meggie's ear. "No signal." She lifted her cell phone.

A board creaked near the window. Something squeaked. Meggie held her breath. The rug. They didn't put the rug back.

"Well, what do we have here?" A man's voice floated through the open window. Light pooled on the ground around Meggie and Beth. They struggled to stand.

"You're not in a hurry to leave, are you?" Meggie heard a click. "I wouldn't if I were you."

"Jason." Beth's voice shook. "Put it down."

Jason crawled through the window and held the gun on Meggie and Beth. "I don't think you're in any position to tell me what to do." He aimed the light at their eyes. "Show me your hands." He landed on the ground with a thump. "Keep 'em up where I can see 'em." He poked the gun at Meggie. "Get in the shack. Move it."

Chapter 46

J ASON KICKED THE DOOR SHUT. "Arms up." He laid the flashlight on the table and frisked Meggie. "Sit down." He pushed her towards the center of the room.

Meggie backed away from Jason and lowered herself to the floor.

Jason pulled the cell phone out of Beth's pocket. He thrust it in his jeans and shoved her towards Meggie. "Your friend Allie has a big mouth." He kept the gun pointed at Meggie and Beth. "She's not too smart either." He reached up and lifted a lantern off the wall. "You should have seen her face when I walked through the door." He set it on the table and turned the switch. The hazy glow threw his shadow against the wall.

Meggie blinked and looked away from the lantern.

"Lucky for me my meeting got cancelled." He pointed the gun at Beth. "Guess who she was yakkin' to when I came in."

"Did you hurt her?" Beth's voice shook.

Jason didn't answer. He picked up the flashlight and backed into the kitchen. He opened a drawer and flashed the light inside. He slammed the drawer shut. "Where is it?" he mumbled to himself. He wrenched a second drawer so hard it came all the way out and its contents spilled across the wood floor. He swept the light back and forth, bent down and picked something up.

Meggie tried to concentrate and form a plan. She had to think of a way out of the mess they were in.

"Nosin' around." Jason strode toward them. "Gettin' into my business. Just like the old man." He halted, rocked on his boots. "You found my gun, didn't ya?"

Meggie couldn't make out Jason's face because he hovered with his back to the light.

"Did you kill Uncle Bud?" Beth's voice quavered. "And Ronnie?"

"Ronnie threatened to tell the old man what we were doing. He gave me no choice." Jason paced. "The old man started snooping." He halted. "I don't like it when someone gets into my business."

A mouse ran under Meggie's leg, across the floor, and disappeared under the wood heater.

"The old man found out we were growing marijuana." Jason paced. "He had no right to stick his nose in." He lowered his voice. "This is our land. We paid for it." He squatted in front of Beth. "Eric and I planned to make lots of money selling that stuff. The old man spoiled it."

Meggie glimpsed his shirt pocket. Beth's flashlight stuck out of it.

"You should have left it alone." He stood and turned his flashlight on Beth. "Turn around real slow."

The wind whistled outside the open window. Branches snapped and crackled. Meggie jerked her head. A shadow darted past the window.

Jason twisted his neck, backed toward the window. He stuck his head out and flashed the light, stood still and listened.

Meggie held her breath.

"You." He strode to the center of the room and pointed the gun at Meggie. "Behind her."

Meggie attempted to stand.

"Stay on your knees." He handed a roll of duct tape to Meggie. "Wrap her hands real tight."

Meggie didn't move.

Jason raised the gun. "Wrap 'em, I said."

Meggie took Beth's hands. She wound the tape around them and sat back.

"Now her mouth."

Meggie's muscles tensed. She unwound the duct tape, bit down and ripped a chunk of tape off the roll. She pressed it over Beth's mouth.

Jason ordered Meggie to stand and pulled her to the table. He set the gun down and taped her hands and mouth. He walked over to Beth and yanked her to a standing position. "We're taking a little ride." He motioned toward the door. "Get in the back of the truck."

Jason yanked at the tailgate and dropped it. He pointed the gun at Meggie. "You first."

Meggie lifted her leg and Jason shoved her from behind. She landed face down on the metal truck bed, rolled over and wormed her way toward the cab of the truck.

Beth rolled in after Meggie.

Jason followed Beth into the back of the truck and bound her ankles with duct tape. He grabbed Meggie's ankles and bound them, too. He jumped out of the truck and slammed the gate shut. Seconds later the driver's door banged and the engine fired up.

Meggie struggled to sit up but fell back against the cab and closed her eyes. Something clattered onto the bed of the truck. She jerked to attention, watched someone mount the tailgate and crawl over. The truck lurched forward.

"It's me, Shirley." A low voice croaked. "I have my bat."

Meggie swallowed and her eyes grew round. She heard Shirley pat the bed of the truck near Beth and seconds later something ripped.

"Ouch." Beth took a ragged breath. "Pocket knife. Near my right cuff."

Meggie watched the knife glint in the faint moonlight and move back and forth near Beth's ankles. Shirley crawled behind Beth and sliced the duct tape from her hands. She inched toward Meggie and yanked the tape off her mouth. Meggie flinched, felt the burn and took a deep breath. "I've never been so glad to see anyone in my life."

Shirley shushed her. "Don't thank me yet." She sliced the tape on Meggie's hands and feet.

"We have to get out of here." Meggie slunk toward the tailgate.

Shirley's voice cracked. "What if he sees us?"

The truck careened around a corner and flung Shirley into Beth.

Beth rose to her knees and grabbed Shirley. "We have no choice."

The truck braked and Meggie slid backwards. The truck hit a bump, bounced up and down. Meggie crawled to the tailgate. She threw her leg up and slithered over. She dropped to the ground and landed on her butt near the side of the road. She moaned and pushed herself up.

Beth slid over the side of the truck near the back end and dropped down.

Shirley lay stretched across the top of the tailgate and clung on. One leg hung over the side and she tugged on the other leg. The truck wheeled to the left and picked up speed.

Meggie ran after the truck until she couldn't breathe. She bent over and gasped for air.

Beth caught up to her. "What's the matter with Shirley?"

Meggie gasped. "I think she's stuck on the tailgate."

The truck bowled around a corner. Its tail lights faded away.

"I know where he's going." Beth tugged Meggie's arm. "Bottomless Lake. We can head him off."

"I hope you're right."

Moonlight lit the trail to the shack. Meggie turned to Beth. "We have to find the flashlight."

"I'm right behind you," Beth said.

Meggie felt her way around the shack to the bedroom window. She got down on her hands and knees and scoured the ground.

Beth searched along the side of the shack. "I found it." She switched the flashlight on and handed it to Meggie.

"Let's get the Bug," Meggie said.

They retraced their steps to the Bug. Meggie crawled inside and felt for the keys in the ignition.

The passenger door swung open and Beth slid in. "We need to go back and take the right fork."

Meggie wrenched the Bug into gear and backed up. She twisted the steering wheel and stepped on the gas. The car shot forward.

The headlights bounced up and down the trees. Meggie gripped the steering wheel and bounced around the first curve. The Bug tilted. "Hang on," she shouted. "Lean to the right."

"There's the fork." Beth pointed. "If we hurry we can head him off before he gets to the lake."

Meggie twisted her neck. "You sure?"

"I know these roads like the back of my hand."

CHAPTER 47

Brush hung over the road and scraped the side of the Bug. "How much farther?" Meggie's voice shook.

Beth fidgeted. "We're almost to the cut-off."

Meggie maneuvered the Bug around a tree and shifted down. The Bug bounced over the ruts.

"There!" Beth shouted. "Turn right. That road will take us to the lake."

Meggie made a sharp right turn onto a wider logging road and accelerated. The Bug dipped into a hole and threw Meggie against the steering wheel. An owl flapped its wings and flew out of a tree. Meggie peered in her rearview mirror. There were no headlights behind them. "Are you sure this is the short cut?" Meggie hit the brake.

Beth pitched forward.

A deer raised its head, turned tail and loped out of sight.

Meggie threw the car into gear and pressed on. The trees thinned on both sides of the road.

"There it is!" Beth shouted.

Meggie gassed the Bug. Up ahead a body of water rippled under the moonlight. The Bug coasted to a stop in front of Bottomless Lake. "They're not here!" Meggie wailed and turned to Beth. "Are you sure this is the only way Jason could have taken?"

Beth pounded the dashboard. "I'm positive."

Meggie backed the car around. "Then they haven't gotten this far." The Bug lurched forward. At the cut-off it veered right. "There he is!" Meggie slammed on the brakes and flipped the headlights off.

Beth gasped. "What are you doing?"

"The truck's stuck." Several yards ahead two headlights beamed into the ground.

"We can't go running up to it." Beth held onto Meggie's arm. "He's got a gun."

Meggie grabbed the flashlight and swung her legs out of the Bug. "We can't sit here, either." She inched toward the truck, her tread light.

Beth caught up to Meggie and tugged her arm. "Hear that?" she whispered.

Meggie cocked her ear. "Yes." The whimper grew louder.

"Over there." Beth pointed toward the back of the truck.

"Shirley?" Meggie panned the area with her flashlight.

Shirley stumbled into the light and staggered near the side of the truck.

Meggie dashed toward her. "Are you hurt?"

"He didn't know I was armed." She leaned against the truck and dangled the aluminum bat. "I think I killed him." She looked dazed and reached into her pocket. "I kept trying 911 but I couldn't get through." She held out her cell phone.

Meggie snatched the phone and handed it to Beth. "Try to make a connection." She turned to Shirley. "Where's Jason?"

Shirley jerked her head to the side. "Back there. He got out of the truck to check on you and Beth when the truck got stuck."

Jason lay on the ground. Meggie knelt down and grabbed the gun that had fallen next to him. She placed her hand on his neck. "He's alive." She scrambled to her feet.

Beth hurried towards Meggie. "I got through," she panted. "They're on their way."

CHAPTER 48

B ETH PLANS TO STAY AT BUD'S until things settle down." Meggie looked at Walter and laid the phone in the cradle. "She's meeting me at the house." Meggie worried Beth hadn't taken enough time to recuperate. It had only been two days since they arrested Jason. "There's bad news."

"Positive identification?" Walter leaned against the counter.

"Yes. Dental records."

A tear formed in Walter's eye and rolled down his cheek. "Bud Anderson shot to death."

Meggie threw her arms around him and pulled him close. "We'll miss Bud." She touched the tear with her finger. "You take it easy today."

Walter took a deep breath. "What about the gun?"

Meggie picked up her car keys. "When the ballistics report comes back, they'll tie it to Jason's gun." She hesitated. "I'm sure."

Walter sniffed. "I hope you're right."

"I better scoot. I'm going to work at the shop after I pick up my things." She started for the door. "You gonna be okay?"

"I'm fine."

Peppie sat on the front step. Meggie bent down and scratched him behind the ear. "See you later."

The redheaded woodpecker greeted Meggie when she arrived at Bud's house. Like a jackhammer it drummed its beak against the dead tree. She stood by the car and watched the head jerk from side to side, up and down.

The front door swung open. "Come on in," Beth called.

Meggie crossed the yard.

Beth gave Meggie a hug and nodded at the woodpecker. "That darn bird—he likes a lot of attention."

"He's a noisy one." Meggie could see Beth had been crying. "How are you doing?"

Beth lifted her hands. "As well as can be expected."

"It won't take me long to pack," Meggie said.

"Would you like something to drink?"

Meggie hesitated.

"I could make coffee or tea."

"I better not. I've had enough caffeine today."

"I haven't." Beth strode towards the kitchen. "As a matter of fact, I think I need a good strong cup of coffee."

"I'm working today at the shop," Meggie said on her way to the bedroom. "But I'm available tomorrow if you need anything."

Meggie emptied the dresser drawers and closet. She picked her book off the nightstand and slid it into her purse.

"Meggie!" Beth cried. "Come here."

Meggie set her bag and painting equipment by the front door and hustled into the kitchen. "What?"

Beth held an envelope in her left hand and a photograph in the other.

"Those are my Key West pictures," Meggie said.

"This is a picture of Jason." Beth held it out to Meggie.

"Jason?" Meggie took the photograph. "This is Jason?" Adrenaline tingled through her body. "This is a panhandler in Key West." She covered her mouth with her hand.

Beth bit her lip. "Let's sit down."

Meggie pulled out a chair and sat down at the table.

Beth wrung her hands and admitted Jason had been panhandling for a couple years in Key West. "The city cracked down on panhandlers, but that didn't stop Jason."

Meggie's mouth opened and closed and she tried to wrap her mind around what Beth told her.

"An easy way to make a buck." Beth's shoulders slumped. "I'm not proud to say I knew that and still loved him."

"Is that how he paid his share for the land?"

Beth nodded.

"Did Ronald know Jason panhandled?"

"Not at first." Beth gazed out the window. "He found out after he sold them the land." She turned back. "He dealt mostly with Eric."

Meggie focused in on the photograph. "Is this chain and medal he's wearing the same one you showed me?" She handed the picture to Beth.

"Chain and medal?" Beth took a close look at the picture. Her face lit up. "I'm sure it is, and there's a date on this photo."

"Ronald died after that picture was taken." Meggie paused. "Didn't he tell you he lost the medal before Ronnie died?"

"He said he lost it a couple months before Ronnie died." Beth's smile faded.

"What's wrong?"

A crow cawed outside the window.

"This photo is good news." Beth pinched the bridge of her nose. "But I have bad news, too." She looked at Meggie. "Allie's gone."

"Gone?" Meggie stared at Beth.

"With Eric."

CHAPTER 49

DETECTIVE BULLDOG LUMBERED IN and shut the door. He spun a large black chair around, sat down and scooted up to the desk. He shoved a small pile of papers to the side.

There was a knock on the door and Bulldog twisted his neck. "Come in."

Deputy Jimmy Fossen, Belle Fossen's son, peeked in. "Sorry to interrupt, but you said you wanted this a.s.a.p." He handed Bulldog a sheet of paper.

Bulldog looked at it and set it on the pile of papers. "Thanks."

Jimmy backed out of the office and nodded at Meggie. His eyes rested on Beth.

"Now, ladies." Bulldog crossed his arms across his chest. "What can I do for you?"

Beth cleared her throat. "It's about my cousin's murder."

Bulldog dipped his chin slightly.

"I know Jason murdered Ronnie," Beth said.

Bulldog held up his hand. "We went over this before. There's nothing—"

"Just a minute." Meggie dug in her purse and pulled out an envelope. She handed a picture across the desk to Bulldog.

Bulldog looked from Meggie to Beth. He rested his arms on the desk and brought the photograph close to his face. "And this is?" He snapped the photograph with his finger.

"That's Jason Williams." Beth shuffled her feet. "When he panhandled in Key West."

Bulldog rubbed his chin and his eyes grew round.

Beth pointed out the medal around his neck and the date on the picture.

Bulldog laid the photo down, took hold of the computer mouse and jiggled it. The monitor lit up.

Meggie peeked at the screen.

Bulldog turned the monitor to the left. "Confidential," he said and left clicked the mouse a couple times.

Meggie watched his eyes dart from side to side.

Bulldog drummed the desk with his fingers and sat back. "Mind if I keep the photograph?"

Meggie nodded. "Please do."

Bulldog stared at the mouse and pushed it in a circle with his finger tip. He looked up and shoved his chair back. "I'll see what I can find out."

Meggie and Beth thanked him and turned to go.

"One more thing." Bulldog leaned back in his chair. "You have any idea where to find Eric Williams?"

CHAPTER 50

THE BIRCH TREE STOOD NAKED against the gray October sky. The cabin birdfeeder dangled and swayed gently in the breeze. Dark golden leaves blanketed the ground beneath it. A chickadee sang and floated down to the feeder. It snatched a sunflower seed and flew to the top of the bare lilac tree. Meggie closed her eyes and inhaled the earthy smell of autumn.

The glass door glided open and Walter stepped onto the deck. "Mind if I join you?"

"Not at all." Meggie slid her chair over. "Indian summers. I love them."

Walter set his camo mug on the table and brushed dried leaves from the deck chair. "Lydia called."

Meggie turned toward Walter. "Any news?"

"Things aren't looking good for Jason. They'll most likely charge him with Ronald's murder, too."

Meggie pressed her palm to her heart. "Thank heavens." The breeze stirred a dead leaf. It rose in the air then swirled to the ground. "I think it was that photo of Jason."

"The red bandana they found by the pool. That was the link," Walter said.

Meggie nodded. "The DNA will come back a match. Jason must have killed Bud the day he went missing." She looked at Walter. "I believe Bud was at the shack. Jason killed him and drove the four-wheeler to Bud's house."

"And he parked it outside the shed." Walter nodded at Meggie and looked away. "You were right. Bud would have locked it up tight."

"Jason drove the truck to the shack." Meggie's eyes pierced the woods and she grew silent.

"Something must have prompted Bud to finally take action," Walter said.

"I think Bud suspected all along that the Williams boys were up to no good."

"Eric must know something. Maybe they'll find him." Walter drained his cup and looked at Meggie. "I shouldn't have to say this—again—but I think it's time you retire from housesitting. Your luck is going to run out one of these days."

"Shirley believes Robert the Doll cursed her."

"I don't know about that, but Shirley and I agree on one thing," Walter said.

Meggie put her finger to her lip and lowered her eyebrows. "Mmm. Let me guess. I shouldn't housesit?"

"Now you're being sarcastic." Walter stood. "I'm heading to the Legion. You have anything planned for today?"

"I'm staying home." Meggie pointed to a chickadee perched on the edge of the deck. "I need to make arrangements for Vera's birthday lunch."

"Where are you taking her?"

"We thought Roadside Inn might be a nice change."

"Is Eldon going along?" Walter asked.

"No men." Meggie grinned. "Chicks only."

"That's my Meggie. Keep the spirit." Walter gave her a peck on the cheek. He slid the glass door open.

"Walter?"

Walter twisted his neck and looked at Meggie. "Huh?"

"Don't forget our square dancing lesson tomorrow."

Walter shuddered.

"You promised." Meggie narrowed her eyes. "Don't try to promenade out of it."

CHAPTER 51

THE NEXT EVENING MEGGIE WALKED into the front room and snapped her jacket. "Walter." She edged up to the recliner and picked up the remote.

"Okay, already." Walter pushed himself up and stomped into the bathroom.

Meggie followed him and stood in the doorway. "You should have told me. I didn't know you hated the idea so much."

Walter frowned. "You know I don't like to dance." He combed his hair and checked the top of his head in the mirror. "Next thing you'll have me wearing cowboy boots."

Meggie smiled. "I like the haircut." She pinched his arm. "And your little bald spot."

Walter trudged to the hallway closet and slipped his coat on. "May as well get this over with. Just hope none of the guys find out."

Meggie laughed. "They will when we go public."

"I said I'd take lessons but I didn't say anything about dancing in public."

Walter brought his truck to a stop in front of Pine Lake Elementary School, the other half of Pine Lake High School. "We're here." He looked at the school but didn't move.

Meggie chuckled. "You're not attending your execution." She jabbed Walter in the ribs. "We're not talking about lessons forever, only four weeks."

"Until the middle of November?" Walter slunk in his seat. "Oh, no. Not during deer hunting." He tugged the bill of his cap down. "I'm not gonna miss deer hunting for some—"

"They're postponing the final lessons until after deer hunting," Meggie sniffed. "We wouldn't want you men to get all bent out of shape."

Later that evening Meggie followed Walter out of the school. "That wasn't so bad, was it?" A light mist moistened her face. She ducked her head and hurried after him.

"No comment," Walter called over the cab.

Meggie buckled up, took her phone out and listened to a voice message.

The driver's door slammed. Walter shook a tissue and wiped the mist from his eyeglasses. "Who called?" He waited for a reply.

"MYOB." Meggie smirked.

"Now who sounds like Shirley?" Walter licked his finger and marked the air.

"Whatever happened to privacy?"

Walter turned the windshield wiper switch. *Schwump schwump schwump.* "You gave up your privacy when you got hitched."

"Can those wipers get any louder?" Meggie asked and punched in a phone number. "Hi Beth. It's Meggie. What's going on?"

Walter turned the wipers off and leaned closer to Meggie.

"Tonight?" Meggie gazed out the cab window. "Walter and I are just leaving Pine Lake." She glanced at the clock under the dash. "I'll be there before 10:00."

Walter pushed his glasses back. "I won't ask questions." He kept his eyes on the road. "You going to tell me?"

"Sorry. I promised not to tell." She dropped her cell phone into her purse and looked at Walter. "I *can* tell you I'm driving out to see Beth."

Walter fell silent.

Meggie watched the light mist sprinkle the windshield and Walter turned the wipers back on. *Schwump schwump schwump.*

The truck rolled to a stop in front of the garage. Meggie pulled her car keys from her purse and climbed out of the truck. "I won't be late," she called over her shoulder.

Walter followed her to the Bug. "Did Beth tell you what it's about?"

"I couldn't tell you if she did." Meggie unlocked the car. "But she didn't."

"Hmm. Big secret?"

Meggie kissed Walter's cheek. "She just said it was important and to hurry."

Walter pushed the driver's door closed after Meggie crawled in. The Bug's engine kicked in and the windshield wipers came on. Walter peered at Meggie and tapped the driver's window.

Meggie cracked it.

"You sure you want to go alone?"

"Yes." Meggie hugged her shoulders. "Beth told me to tell you . . ." She turned the wipers off.

"What?"

Meggie grew serious. "Don't tell anyone where I'm going."

"I don't know who I'd tell." Walter shook his head and saluted. "Call if you need me."

The Bug rolled down the drive. Meggie turned the heater up and glanced in the rearview mirror. Walter walked through the front door and the ceiling light came on. She turned onto the street and the reflection vanished. Meggie didn't need the rearview mirror to tell her what Walter did next. She would bet a dollar to a donut hole he sat down in his recliner, picked up the remote and turned the boob tube on.

Meggie drove the speed limit but kept an eye out for deer. She decreased her speed on the dirt road. Before long she turned onto the gravel drive. The yard light glowed through the trees. She pulled up in front of the house and killed the engine. A soft light filtered through the curtain next to the front door.

The wind whistled and the trees shivered. Meggie pulled her jacket close, climbed the front steps and rapped on the screen door.

Beth pulled the wooden door back and pushed the screen door open. "Thanks for coming." She pulled Meggie into the room. "Let's go into the kitchen."

Meggie's eyes darted around the room. "Has something happened?" She noted all the curtains were closed.

"Please, sit down." Beth pulled out a kitchen chair.

Meggie slipped her jacket off and hung it on back of the chair.

Beth tucked a strand of hair behind her ear. "I'll be right back." She strode into the large bedroom and closed the door.

Voices murmured, a bed squeaked and the bedroom door opened. "Meggie?"

Meggie looked up.

"These are my friends." A young couple followed Beth into the kitchen. "Allie and Eric." They sat down next to Beth. "I need your help to convince them to go to the authorities." Beth laid her hand on Allie's shoulder. "Tell them they can't keep running."

Meggie's skin tingled. She recognized Eric from the casino, the blackjack dealer. She smiled at them and wondered what they were running from. As far as she knew they weren't suspects but only wanted for questioning.

Beth looked at Eric. "Tell her."

Eric took a deep breath. "I didn't have anything to do with Bud's death." He squeezed Allie's hand. "I can't lie and say I never suspected Jason had something to do with it." A tear rolled down his cheek and he wiped it away. "I hated myself for thinking that way about my own brother."

"Why did you suspect him?"

"Jason knew Bud had been nosing around." Eric rubbed his hand on his leg. "He discovered four-wheeler tracks on our land. He figured sooner or later Bud would find our marijuana."

"Tell me about the marijuana." Meggie leaned forward.

"We bought the land for hunting." Eric met Meggie's eyes. "Jason got the bright idea from a friend to plant marijuana and sell it." He hung his head. "I made the mistake of going along with it."

"You took care of it while Jason lived in Key West?"

"We didn't plant it until last summer." Eric straightened his back. "We never sold the stuff. We destroyed it after Bud started getting suspicious."

"What about Ronnie?" Meggie's stomach tightened.

Allie put her arm around Eric and rubbed his back.

"I don't know anything about Ronnie's murder." Eric took a deep breath and looked at Beth. "But I think Jason does. I'm sorry, Beth."

Meggie glanced at Allie and Eric. "Why did you run?"

"That was my fault." A flush crept across Allie's cheeks. "I figured Jason would try to save his own skin and blame Eric for Bud's murder." She looked at Eric. "You know he'd turn on you." She closed her eyes. "Running was a dumb thing to do."

"I'm guilty of growing marijuana." Eric's chin trembled. "But I'm not guilty of murder."

"You have a choice." Meggie set her elbows on the table. "You can run but they'll find you sooner or later."

"I know." Eric looked at Allie.

"They'll go harder on you if you keep running." Meggie set her jaw.

"Allie had nothing to do with any of this." Eric pulled her close. "She didn't know about the marijuana either."

"Then turn yourselves in." Meggie tapped the table. "Tell the authorities what you've just told me."

Eric covered his eyes.

"How did you get here?" Meggie lowered her voice.

"His car's in the woods." Beth fidgeted. "I told them to hide it."

Allie rubbed Eric's arm. "He knows he'll have to testify against Jason." She looked at Meggie. "It won't be easy."

"Let's go." Eric pushed his chair back and held his hand out toward Allie. "You coming?"

CHAPTER 52

A WEEK LATER MEGGIE ARRIVED at Hearts and Flowers Gift Shop. The bell tinkled above the door and Meggie called, "Greetings!"

Shirley marched through the break room curtain with Audrey on her heels. "We thought you would never get here." She feigned impatience.

Meggie closed the door. "What do you mean?" She held her arm up and tapped her wristwatch. "I'm early."

Vera stood near the counter with her head bent close to Eldon's. She looked up and smiled.

"Happy birthday." Meggie sidled close and embraced her.

"Thank you, dear." She clutched Meggie's hand. "I believe this is going to be the happiest birthday I've had in a long while." She blushed and peeked sideways at Eldon. "Lunch with friends and an evening with my gentleman."

Meggie caught a certain look. "Are you planning something special, Eldon?"

He nodded at Vera. "Surprise plans for my little lady." He patted her hand. "You go on now and enjoy your birthday lunch."

On the way to Shirley's Taurus, Vera whispered to Meggie, "He's such a dear man." Her eyes lit up and she giggled. "I think I've fallen in love. Imagine, at my age."

The drive to Roadside Inn seemed unusually long. Meggie noticed Audrey's knuckles had turned white from holding the side of the car door. She understood her fear. Shirley's driving seemed to be getting worse, plus she had a lead foot. Meggie felt a measure of relief when she heard the turn signal click on and off. *And she worries about Nettie's driving.*

Shirley cranked the wheel to the right and drove through the parking lot. She looked right and left and chugged into a vacant spot at the end of the first row. "We're here, girls."

Meggie's seat belt clicked. She crawled out of the car and the wind whipped her face. She pulled the front passenger door open and helped Vera out.

"I haven't been to Roadside Inn in ages." Vera slid her purse over her arm and her coat flapped in the wind. "This is so much fun."

The hostess greeted the women and led them through the dining room to a window table. "What a lovely view." Vera set her purse down on the floor. "I never tire of our beautiful lakes."

Meggie watched the blue-gray water froth and pulled out a chair. "Sand Lake looks rough today." Glasses clinked and waitresses rushed back and forth. "They're busy," Meggie said and looked at the customers.

A young woman dressed in jeans and a plaid button-down shirt stopped at the table. She slid her arm around Vera.

The women grew quiet and all eyes turned on the attractive young woman.

Vera's mouth fell open. "Molly. What a nice surprise. It's been too long."

"I know. I don't get into Pine Lake very often anymore."

"Molly Riley." Vera took the young woman's hand. "I'd like you to meet Audrey Peterson, Shirley Wright and Meggie Moore. They're treating me to a birthday lunch."

"It's nice meeting you, ladies." Molly turned toward Meggie. "You housesat at Bud Anderson's, right?"

Meggie nodded.

"I thought the world of Bud," Molly said. "I still can't believe he's gone."

"Molly and Michael have a small hobby farm not far from Bud's place," Vera said. "A pretty yellow house."

Meggie recalled the small yellow farmhouse nestled on a rolling hill and the shiny black horse.

"I talked to him the day before he went missing to see if everything was all right," Molly said.

"What do you mean?" Meggie asked.

"The Williams boys were driving by our place an awful lot. I thought it was odd. When I spotted smoke down that way, I called Bud."

Meggie thought a minute. "Bud must have known they were destroying the marijuana. Maybe that was the straw that broke the camel's back and Bud confronted them."

The waitress approached the table. "I better let you ladies eat," Molly said and patted Vera's shoulder. "Have a happy birthday."

Molly turned to go but halted. "Meggie, would you consider housesitting our hobby farm? If you like to ride, my horses are gentle."

Meggie could feel Shirley's disapproval.

Molly continued. "My husband works in North Dakota and I'd like to drive out and spend some time with him."

Meggie thought a minute. "I would love to housesit your hobby farm." She shot Shirley a defiant look. "You work out the details and let me know."

"That meal was wonderful." Vera sat back in her chair. "I'm completely satisfied." She lifted her water glass and looked over Meggie's shoulder.

Meggie turned her head.

The waitress set a small cake down in the center of the table. "Happy birthday," she said.

"Oh, my goodness." Vera clasped her hands.

Meggie cut the cake and handed Vera a piece. She noticed Molly and another young woman get up from a booth and walk toward the cashier. "Molly seemed pleased to see you." Meggie handed a piece of cake to Audrey and Shirley.

"Molly's grandmother and I were such good friends." She shook her head. "She's gone now, poor dear." Vera patted her mouth with her napkin and smiled. "That young lady has such an imagination. She actually believes her house is haunted."

All eyes turned toward Vera.

"Haunted?" Meggie asked and set her fork down.

Fred Jackson built the house years ago," Vera said. "He and Bud were good friends."

"Is Fred still around?" Meggie asked.

Vera's eyes widened. "I'm afraid not. One day he just up and disappeared. No one ever heard from him again."

CHAPTER 53

THE FOLLOWING DAY MEGGIE carried a shopping bag into the house. She set it on the floor and took out a large box.

The bathroom door slammed and Walter walked into the kitchen. "What did you buy now?" He scratched his head.

Meggie lifted the cover off the box, reached in and brought out a brown leather cowboy boot. She raised it in front of her.

Walter arched his eyebrows. "Going western on me?" Peppie meowed at Walter's feet. He bent down and stroked him.

Meggie inhaled the raw scent of leather and ran her finger down the boot. "One never knows what adventure lies ahead or around the corner," she said, thinking about Molly's black horse. "Maybe you should buy a pair of cowboy boots, too. We can ride the range together."

Walter looked at her but didn't move. "I have no idea what in the blazes you're talking about." He tapped the side of his head. "My train doesn't run on the same tracks."

Meggie laughed. "Your train is boring." She took the other boot from the box. "I thought you might want to add horseback riding to your bucket list."

"Horseback riding. Cowboy boots." Walter shook his head. "After two murders and one wild ride through the woods hog-tied in the back of a pick-up, you need a good pair of slippers, not cowboy boots." Walter chuckled and ambled into the front room still shaking his head. He sat down on the recliner, picked up the remote control and flipped the channel on the boob tube.

Acknowledgments

Thank you, fellow writers, for your inspiration; my daughter Jackie for "refreshing my memory" of Key West; Shawn D. Smith, Key West City Attorney; Bogdan "Bob" Vitas, Jr., Key West City Manager; Angela Foster, editor; Joey Halvorson, photographer; and North Star Press.

A special thanks to Five Wings Arts Council for awarding me grants, with funds from the McKnight Foundation supplemented with Legacy funds, to further my knowledge of writing.